Within the inner sanctum . . .

"Sowhat Dihje here."

"I need Mr. Holmes."

"This is regrettable. Master is elsewhere. Who is needing this, please?"

"This is Harrington. Wilkesford Harrington. There is an emergency. My son-in-law has been shot. He's been murdered."

"Ah! Master undoubtedly will express interest. Murder is most curious to him."

"Can you reach him?"

"He will come within soon. Touch nothing. Have a good day."

Mr. Dihje gently replaced the instrument. As silently as he had come he crossed the room, passed under the massive head of a charging bull elephant, twisted an ornate brass handle, and disappeared through polished double oak doors. . . .

SAN FRANCISCO KILLS

BY
DENNY MARTIN FLINN

BANTAM BOOKS
NEW YORK • TORONTO • LONDON • SYDNEY • AUCKLAND

SAN FRANCISCO KILLS
A Bantam Book / January 1991

ISBN 0-553-28044-9

Published simultaneously in the United States and Canada

Bantam Books are published by Bantam Books, a division of Bantam
Doubleday Dell Publishing Group, Inc. Its trademark, consisting of the
words "Bantam Books" and the portrayal of a rooster, is Registered in
U.S. Patent and Trademark Office and in other countries. Marca
Registrada. Bantam Books, 666 Fifth Avenue, New York, New York
10103.

PRINTED IN THE UNITED STATES OF AMERICA

RAD   0 9 8 7 6 5 4 3 2 1

Part I

Chapter 1

The episode of the marriage moratorium.

Almost all of the guests thought it a fine day for a wedding. The sky was a crystalline blue. White clouds drifted by in a pretty parade. The fourteen-acre estate was immaculately polished. Beyond the terra-cotta terrace, the bay was dotted with weekend sailors. By the time two hundred of the city's finest families had gathered, the sun had mopped up the customary morning dampness. By the time they had settled in rented chairs on the appropriate side of a flower-festooned aisle, it had risen gracefully overhead and reflected in no one's eyes. The bridal party slowly wended their way along an aromatic path and onto the platform, where they formed a stately tableau. The guests gazed enviously upon the radiant face of the bride. The priest dramatically intoned the order for the solemnization of marriage.

". . . he has instructed those who enter into this relation to cherish each other's infirmities and weaknesses, to comfort each other in sickness, trouble, and sorrow, in honesty and industry to provide for each other, to pray for and encourage each other in the things which pertain to God, and to live together as the heirs of the grace of life."

The assembly sat patiently motionless. The bay wind was soft and fragrant.

"Forasmuch as these two Persons have come hither to be made one in this holy estate, if there be any here present who knows any just cause why they may not lawfully be joined in marriage, I require him now to make it known, or ever after to hold his peace."

It was at this moment that someone expressed the belief that a wedding was not, in fact, the most appropriate event for that gentle Sunday afternoon in that Golden City which serves as a haven for so many eccentric opinions. None more eccentric, indeed, than one being expressed at that time.

For at that precise moment a shot rang out and the groom, heretofore standing splendidly straight in a custom-tailored Pierre Cardin cutaway, with the light of love and propriety shining in his eyes, fell dead at the white satin-shod feet of his intended.

Chapter 2

During which little is accomplished.

Needless to say, this was the cause of no modest alarm. Cries and whispers filled the air, following hard upon the heels of one of those pregnant silences which are the natural result of sudden and unexpected events. Initially no one wished to be the first to break the stillness. Eventually the assemblage was plunged into chaos. Here is how the audience's reaction wound so rapidly from the former to the latter:

The immediate instinct of the majority was to turn to their neighbors with an expression of puzzlement. A sense of the sinister settled on the gathering.

This foreboding was, then, increased to an almost intolerable level by the singular sound of a high-pitched female scream which split the silence sharply, cleaved it, one might say, like a finely honed chopper brought suddenly to bear on a tender piece of liver, the immediate effect of which was the releasing of a floodgate of confusion and anxiety.

Anxiety was to be found in greater proportions toward the front of the assembly. Confusion increased according to the distance of the guests from the supine (but still handsome) groom. If truth be told, those furthest from the event, whose ability to follow the proceedings was hampered by various factors (including the inaudible mumbling of the representative of the Protestant church and the general outdoors), had not been paying much attention. This is a standard feature of these ceremonies and ordinarily of no consequence. In this case, however, a large proportion of the assembly was now left with no concrete understanding of what, if anything, had taken place up front. Nevertheless, they became equally frantic.

The bride, kneeling over the body of her fiancé, and presumably in a state of shock, made repeated attempts to rouse him. Since she had never before (surprising though it may be in this new world of premarital freedom) been required to execute that intimate morning-after maneuver, her blandishments were as awkward as they were ineffective.

The mother of the bride, easily the most excitable member of the family and the person responsible for that first memorable *geshraye* had followed that active contribution with the simple expedient of passing out. This now placed not one but two bodies on the platform, and as both were still immobile when those members of the crowd from the far reaches of the grouping managed to work themselves into a more advantageous position for viewing, it served only to heighten both the confusion and the anxiety.

The father of the bride (much to the benefit of the forward momentum of this narrative) took the initiative. His features indicated that, although suffering the shock of disbelief that was universal among the immediate standees, he was one of the first to absorb what had actually taken place. This may have been due to the fact that he was a man of very considerable activity and was accustomed to leadership; it may have been due to the fact that in the few moments sandwiched between the groom's inconvenient death and his future mother-in-law's impersonation of same, the father drew on his reserve of calm and excellence of eyesight to notice a thin trickle of blood appearing behind the right ear of the groom; or it may have been due to the fact that, owing to his complete inability to accept his daughter's assessment of the charms and potential of her beloved, he was, upon calculating the results of the event, extremely relieved. In all charity, we might assign this last to the not unusual experience of a proud father being forced to turn over the protection of his little girl to the inexperienced arms of a relative newcomer. (Then again, and also in all charity, the boy had been a boob). At any rate, the father of the bride now turned on his heels abruptly and set out across the lawn for the house, where he might sooner communicate with whatever authorities had both jurisdiction and experience in these matters.

The priest did nothing. He still wore the same expression with which he had warned the young couple of the dangerous pitfalls of an unknown future and spelled out for them the rewards of a lifetime of happy companionship. Among the huge assemblage, he alone appeared unmoved. Perhaps he consid-

ered the catastrophe to be some sort of sign from God. Or
perhaps he was serenely awaiting one.

The general alarm, having been passed back like waves from
a water-skier's trough, eventually became a hubbub of excite-
ment the likes of which have seldom been seen in the quiet,
pine-shrouded community of Belvedere. In the audience was
more than one young man who had (until now) envied the
position occupied by the groom, and had hoped to gain for
himself the multitude of advantages that would accompany it.
Others in the assembly had been calculating the effect on their
own fortunes which the merger of two such prominent families
augured. None among the rest of the cast exhibited any distin-
guishing behavior, so they need not, individually, concern us at
this time.

The crush of onlookers pressed forward. Over four hundred
people, no matter how docile and well-mannered, can quickly
become a dangerous mob. Small children wearing their Sunday
best were snatched up to their parents' breasts. Teenage girls in
unaccustomed high heels tottered uneasily as the crowd unac-
countably shifted in various directions. Young men who felt the
need to impress pushed their way forward, jostling the crowd
and adding to the restlessness. Senior citizens gossiped loudly.
And as the murmur of "murder" swept like lightning here and
there, the group became more and more volatile. It had just
reached the boiling point, when one unknown but hardy soul
took it upon himself to announce his own rash conclusions to
all, and his booming baritone shouted some unintelligible but
exhortatory warning of present danger. That did it. A stampede
got under way. With some participants pushing forward and
some pushing back, with some pushing in and some pushing
out, with some losing sight of others they suddenly felt the need
to be near, the blue-blooded guests became a panicked and
directionless herd. When too many pounds of frantic flesh
mounted the wedding platform in order to escape the danger of
being trampled underfoot, it collapsed with a prolonged
splintering sound. Thus the general scene was, in short order,
reduced to complete chaos. Underscored by cacophonous
screaming. This went on for some time. The groom disappeared
under the packed and tumultuous bodies, but as he was already
deceased, all this did him no harm. Fortunately when events

were sorted out, it happened that no one else was seriously injured.

Nothing further to be gained from these extras, we shall follow that one member of the principal cast who found sufficient reserve of character to leg it to the nearest telephone.

Chapter 3

In which the father of the bride sets the proverbial ball rolling.

Mr. Wilkesford Harrington had "interests." Not as in stamp collecting, gourmet cooking, jogging, or golf; as in shipping companies, malls, computer-supply firms, restaurant chains. He was on a number of Boards of Directors. Although he was never in the news, and his name was not on the letterhead of a major company, he wielded enormous influence in more than a few of America's plushest conference rooms. He was a man who in another country might have been designated not Mr. but Sir, for surely his business ruthlessness, political astuteness, and philanthropic tax dodges would have combined to make him the recipient of benign recognition. And he was not a man accustomed to dealing with the lower echelons of any bureaucracy. Nor was he a man who failed to recognize the usefulness of private telephone numbers. Accordingly, and in spite of it being a Sunday afternoon, he was able to immediately initiate a conversation with his Congressman. (And when we say "his," we mean this literally.) This resulted in the dispatchment of a carful of detectives, an ambulance of paramedics, a photographic and forensic team, a small detachment of shield-wielding, riot-trained, uniformed policemen, six patrol cars, two Doberman pinschers trained to sniff out illegal chemical substances, and the county medical examiner and his assistant, arriving last in that automobile commonly referred to among their associates as the Meat Wagon. (The majority of personnel were borrowed for the event from neighboring communities and the county sheriff's office, the Belvedere police themselves being unable to field a full-size volleyball team.)

Among this small army were any number of qualified, if insufficiently intuitive, professionals. Upon their arrival, however, the indirection continued. The wedding party gesticulated. The servants aided. The crowd milled, now intensely gregarious, as if they were making up for having been struck speechless earlier. Little by little, however, a form suggested itself. This was entirely the result of the efforts of Chief Shareen Kelly, a woman whose statuesque, redheaded beauty so disarmed her underlings that she was in the well-worn habit of having to constantly repeat her instructions.

Chief Kelly had been a member of the Belvedere police force for two years, following eight years on the larger San Francisco force, which followed directly upon her graduation from the academy, where she gained excellent marks. (This in spite of a slight prejudice against women which she had to contend with there, and a slight condescension toward particularly good-looking women with which she had had to contend her entire life.) Now, in her continuing effort to improve her lot in life, she was attending law school in the evenings, not to practice law, but to improve her resume and become qualified for even loftier positions in the hierarchy of criminal investigation. Ms. Kelly was ambitious, talented, and—in the opinion of her staff —somewhat bossy. She was discreetly aware of this latter tendency, and was attempting to mitigate it recently. On the other hand, the rampant disorder she found upon arriving at the scene, and the number of unguided public employees who had arrived—presumably roused from their quiet Sunday by the same call from the Congressman that she had received—obviously required quick and confident handling.

She set the patrolmen to sealing off the estate and herding the assemblage. She set the paramedics to the task of Mrs. Harrington, spying instantly that it would require at least three of them to heft the woman's inactive bulk. She set the photographic and forensic team to examine the body, which they shared with the attention of the coroner. She conferred with the other detectives, and launched an immediate investigation of the area. The detectives moved outward in concentric circles from that spot known throughout criminology and literary circles alike as the Scene of the Crime until they reached the secure perimeters and linked up with their uniformed brethren.

The Dobermans galloped across the lawn, dragging their trainers, and rushed into the crowd enthusiastically. There they sniffed and tore at the pockets of numerous younger guests until Chief Kelly, realizing that the animals had failed to discern between appropriate and inappropriate clues relative to the case, sent them packing.

Chief Kelly did all this with confidence and clarity, automatically delivering each of her instructions twice. Order was restored. All this resulted, some two hours later, in so little evidence and information that nothing of consequence can be related here.

The father of the bride, retaining his mantle of leadership, circulated with the minions of the law. It was not long before he became aware that, in spite of prodigious feats of fact-gathering, their activity was in no way narrowing in on a satisfactory explanation of the episode. Consequently, he slipped away from the crowd and headed off for a telephone once again. There he made a second call. This one to an individual without title or official status, but in whom he nevertheless placed a great deal more of his trust and to whom he offered his considerable resources. This call was delayed only by the amount of time it took Mr. Harrington to hurry down the hall and enter his private office, where he had access to a more suitable telephone, one that had no other lines and was frequently swept for listening devices. Mr. Harrington was a cautious and careful man.

Chapter 4

In which the affair passes into capable hands.

That second telephone call rang three consecutive times in an inner sanctum set deep in the fog-shrouded hills across the Bay in Pacific Heights. During this interval, a small, neat man with a serene demeanor glided silently across a thick Persian carpet to a miniature surrogate of His Highest Serenity, Buddha, with glowing red eyes, which sat meditatively in the center of the lacquered surface of a Louis Quatorze writing desk. He reached this factotum at the conclusion of the second ring, and stood calmly as the muffled sound emanated softly from the bowels of the Icon. Then he gently lodged his brown right forefinger in the ample belly button. The God made no protest. Instead the middle of His straining midsection separated itself cleanly and exposed a superb contemporary example of that useful invention of Mr. Alexander Graham Bell.

"Sowhat Dihje here."

"I need Mr. Holmes."

"This is regrettable. Master is elsewhere. Who is needing this, please?"

"This is Harrington. Wilkesford Harrington. There is an emergency. My future son-in-law has been shot. He's been murdered."

"Ah! Master undoubtedly will express interest. Murder is most curious to him."

"He ought to be here before the police trample over too much of the evidence. Can you reach him?"

"This is a possible possibility."

"All right. In Belvedere. He knows the house."

"He will come within soon. Touch nothing. Have a good day."

Mr. Dihje gently replaced the instrument and closed the

yawning cavity of the smiling God. As silently as he had come, he crossed the room, passed under the massive head of a charging bull elephant, twisted an ornate brass handle, and disappeared through polished double oak doors.

Chapter 5

Rooms on Baker Street.

Mr. Dihje now hesitated. He was clear on the matter of his employer's principal instruction: disturbance while he was engaged within the confines of the fourth and highest floor of his domain was to be avoided whenever possible. There were any number of demands constant upon the attentions of the peripatetic personality. Mr. Dihje's obligations included sorting them by importance, urgency, and interest.

The fact that solicitations of infinite variety came from numerous avenues was not least due to the fact that his employer —foolishly, in the opinion of Mr. Dihje—insisted on keeping a well-polished brass plaque attached to the brick facade of their mansion. It had been in position for some years now (and often commanded the attention of tourists who plodded the scenic walking tour mapped out in one of the city's most popular guidebooks). It read:

SPENCER HOLMES
Consulting Detective
2210 Baker Street

Spencer, who needed neither the income nor the activity which public advertising generated, and who, in fact, often found anonymity useful, nevertheless insisted the shingle be maintained. It was, he was sure, the exact thing his illustrious grandfather would have been most insistent on, an affirmation that Spencer made himself equally accessible to the various castes and classes of the homogeneous community he inhabited.

Due to this, Mr. Dihje often fielded requests for assistance made directly at the front door. Some of them he denied outright. The serious consulting detective, his employer instructed him, never entangled himself in matrimonial affairs. Didn't, that is, do divorce, or "keyhole," work. For cases which Mr. Dihje deemed suitable, he took the client's particulars, and passed on the information to his boss at the next appropriate opportunity.

But murder was different. Murder, Spencer Holmes had often instructed Mr. Dihje, was the most intriguing, the most final, the most mysterious of all the thousands of sinister activities which constituted the interests of San Francisco's netherworld. It was a crime in which the victim could not speak for himself. As a man who had inherited wealth and brains (and, to be completely unfair about this, good looks), Spencer felt a responsibility to the disenfranchised. There can hardly be a more disenfranchised citizen than the murder victim. And then there were the circumstances: such an affair is almost always a challenge to the rational mind, incomprehensible as it is to a moral man. Murder requires an exhaustive examination of the immediate circumstances for means and opportunity, a task not to be trusted to public servants. Murder often exposed delicate and explosive emotions in the psyche of those involved, emotions which, if caught at the tide, could give significant indication of motive. In other words, murder was unfailingly fascinating to the complicated, penetrating mind of his inscrutable employer. For this reason, and because the deep baritone of the caller had imparted to Sowhat Dihje a feeling of authority, he made his decision in favor of the client.

He moved rapidly. He crossed the shiny black marble floor of the vaulted hall and entered a steam-driven elevator. Working the rope efficiently, he quickly ascended to the roof. He stepped out onto a red-brick terrace that was dotted with fruit trees wrapped in fog. He crossed to a glass facade that fronted ethereal private chambers perched like a benign Berchtesgaden on the Victorian edifice. He gently opened the stained-glass door, and stepped inside.

Then he hesitated once again. Down which avenue would he find his employer? Included in the master's interests were any number of activities requiring apparatuses. To Mr. Dihje's left was the well-padded arena in which Spencer practiced the ancient art of jujitsu. To his right was the glass cupola of the Nero Wolfe room, which housed a large collection of bonsai trees surrounded by other jungle fauna. Further on was the lagoon, where Spencer perfected his Australian crawl or breath-control techniques, and behind that, a music room where he might be at the piano practicing one of Liszt's *Hungarian Rhapsodies,* or even "Totentanz," of which he was so fond.

Mr. Dihje stood still and listened for a clue. He heard the sound of silence, which told him what he needed to know, and he made his decision. He moved swiftly along the hall, turned down an obscure corridor, and ducked under an ornamental archway, until he stood in front of a heavy oak-paneled door. He opened it, and glided quietly across the floor of the small, unadorned room. At its center, upon a rich Oriental carpet, sat his employer in the lotus position. Mr. Dihje bent nearly double and whispered into his ear a summary of the communication he had received from the man known as Harrington. Then he straightened and waited respectfully. In a moment, the closed eyelids of his employer fluttered upwards, revealing penetrating gray eyes (for which, in female circles of Northern California society, he was well known). An expression of interest lit up his face.

"Excellent, my dear Mr. Dihje."

Chapter 6

Meanwhile.

In Belvedere, Wilkesford Harrington put down the telephone and sauntered thoughtfully across his study. That his wife had fainted was of little concern. She was a theatrical and mercurial personality whose response to events was often startling to those unfamiliar with her flamboyance. She was also resilient, however, and he had no doubt that her recovery would be reasonably rapid and complete. Harrington fully expected to hear his wife speculate that the groom would undoubtedly have disappointed their beloved daughter eventually, and to pronounce his failing to fulfill his responsibilities vis-à-vis their wedding as a blessing in disguise. As for his daughter, he had more concern. An equally resilient, if far more dependable, personality, she nevertheless lacked experience with untoward events. To date he had used his considerable wealth, as well as his power and prestige in San Francisco, to shelter her from many of the grimmer aspects of modern life. She was the apple of his eye, and if he was wise enough to know that she had been independent for some time now, he nevertheless still thought of her as —though she would have laughed cynically at this—quite young. This concern was based on the simple fact that what she once was to him, she would always be: Daddy's little girl.

His thoughtful perambulation brought him to the window overlooking the still chaotic pastoral scene. He clasped his hands behind his back, and took on a dark expression.

He saw that the scene had sorted itself out. By three o'clock midafternoon the participants were arranged as follows:

The wedding party was gathered downstairs in the living room of the host. The bride, a straw-haired young beauty with an infectious smile on other occasions, alternated between hysteria and confusion, depending upon her wavering ability to grasp the facts. The mother of the groom, never that member of the family best grounded in reality, kept inquiring as to when the wedding could be expected to proceed and the match consummated. The father of the groom pursued his amateur's interest in music, and picked out a simple jazz motif on the piano. His rented tuxedo jacket now lay on the piano bench beside him, his starched white shirt was open at the collar, and his black bow tie hung loosely around his neck. The mother of the bride was still in a dead faint, sprawled lengthwise on an enormous couch where she had been deposited by the paramedics on their way out. Drifting around the room, eight pairs of ushers and bridesmaids were engaged in that eternal pas de deux known as flirting, made the more difficult, but no less titillating, by circumstances that demanded somber behavior.

The temporary hired help had been herded into the kitchen. Their topic of conversation chiefly consisted of exclamations over the eccentricities of the rich, and the understandable apprehension that under the circumstances they might have some difficulty collecting their day's wages. Various discussion groupings split up into musicians, carhops, bartenders, and maids. The caterers, seeing themselves not as menial labor but independent contractors, kept tightly to themselves and fiercely guarded what remained of the refreshments.

The regular household staff continued to circulate freely, doing whatever they were asked with swift and silent efficiency, as if the event were no different from one of the numerous family gatherings they had attended to in the past.

Of the guests, forty were corralled in the dining room, while the remaining were allowed the run of the terrace. A rumor that this division had been made based upon social status caused a strong undercurrent of resentment to ripple through the crowd. The rumor was false. The patrolmen had simply been instructed to move inside that portion of the assembly that had been seated in the first four rows and that thus might be relied on to give eyewitness accounts of the facts.

And shortly thereafter Spencer Holmes arrived on the scene. He was accompanied, of course, by his faithful retainer.

Chapter 7

At last the investigation begins in earnest.

The first thing Spencer Holmes did was enter into a private conversation with three men whose presence at the celebration had gone undetected. These men were not known to a single member of the household, household staff, wedding party, or any of the guests. Harrington had hired them to attend the wedding, but would not have recognized them on sight. (In fact, there were any number of relatives present Harrington would not have recognized, and for whom, to use his own words, he had little use.) As for the wedding party and guests, everyone present knew someone, but certainly no one knew everyone. Aunt Dorothy, the large, grey-haired woman draped in some homosexual's version of an Arabian caftan, probably had the clearest picture of the complex family bloodlines, but today even this reliable sender of birthday and anniversary cards was overwhelmed. Hence it was a simple thing for the three men to remain incognito throughout the afternoon.

These three men had been invited to the celebration in order to guard against the unfortunate eventualities which were apt to occur in any large gathering of the well-to-do. They were private detectives in plain clothes. They had been sent by an organization with a good deal of experience in the matter, the Pinkertons, and were generically known throughout the San Francisco underworld as Pinks.

They had been quite prepared to deal with pickpockets, for whom they had kept a well-peeled eye since the beginning of the affair. Regarding both the silver service and the enormous pile of household gifts awaiting transfer to the newlyweds' abode, they had been vigilant. They had run the image of each of the various guests and employees through their mental file of bad characters, miscreants, and no-goods. Until now, they had performed exemplary service. Not a suspicious movement or

event had escaped them. Even Cousin Sadie had been quietly
persuaded to replace the pair of Tiffany salt and pepper shakers
that had found their way into her ample purse.

However, one thing was now clear to even those least able to
follow the rapidly unfolding events: the groom had been murdered. This, in all charity, was something fairly unusual, even
in their eccentric profession. Let us hope it will not be held
against them by their employers should the question of references arise in the future.

At any rate, it was these men Spencer sought out immediately upon his arrival. He knew they would be present and,
having delayed his departure long enough to telephone the Pinkerton office, he knew who they would be. Two of them he
found immediately on the terrace. Had he not known their
faces, he would have found them with equal expediency. They
were the only guests present who wore white athletic socks, and
thus were easy to spot in the crowd. The third, who was identified some moments later in the dining room, had the additional
foresight to leave a tuxedo rental tag hanging from the rear of
his jacket.

Their leader, Louis, was a tall, thin man with a concave
chest, a long face with saddlebag cheeks, and lines of age running vertically down from his eyes, which gave the impression
of constant tears. He ambled up to Spencer lethargically but
spoke in rapid sentences without a hitch. After the renewal of
their acquaintance, which had spanned a decade and included
more than one successfully concluded case of mutual interest,
Spencer cut the proverbial cackle and got down to the horses.

"What happened?" he said.

The straightforward approach failed to succeed. In short,
they had not the faintest idea. Since the crowd had attracted a
good deal more of their professional interest than the wedding
party, the three men had purposely stationed themselves in an
inverted triangle pointing away from the center of events. Louis
filled Spencer in on the startling and premature conclusion to
the ceremony, which we have seen for ourselves. Then he went
on to explain his team's own activity.

"Hugo and I ran to the gate and locked it. I left two uniformed guards there. They swore that no one had left the premises since the beginning of the ceremony. They're Pinks, too, so

I think they're pretty reliable. We searched the grounds, circling the perimeter clockwise and counterclockwise, until we met up down there, beneath the terrace. Nobody was around. The fence is twelve feet high, covered with ivy. I figure you couldn't climb it without leaving marks, or being seen from the roof of the house. That's where Delbart went right away. He got up there within a minute and kept an eye peeled. You can see everything from there, except in close to the house. He stayed there until enough of the local cops came to secure the perimeter. Since then, we've been frisking the guests, without them knowing it, of course. We've worked most of the crowd, and no one is carrying hardware. We didn't get a look in the purses, and anybody could have hidden a gun just about anywhere. Except for Harrington, no one detached themselves from the crowd. Then the cops arrived and moved them all up to the terrace and dining room."

While the four of them stalked the full perimeter of the terrace, Spencer listened, his eyes cast on a vague spot on the ground some three feet in front of them, his hands clasped meditatively behind him. His questions, brief and to the point, would have impressed even the hardest-boiled members of his profession.

"The help?"

"All screened by Pinkerton last week, references checked. No sheets, no one in service less than two years, nothing suspicious."

"The gun?"

"Nobody could draw and fire a pistol without being seen, in my opinion."

"Never underestimate the possibility that the unexpected might go overlooked."

"Granted, it's not out of the question. But take a look at the lawn there. The guests were on that side, grouped tightly. The chairs have since been upset. Hardly anyone could get off a clean shot. And not without extending their shooting arm. Two or three in a conspiracy could have covered it up. But here's another thing: a gunshot like that, it would have scared the crap out of the neighbors. But nobody reported anything like that. Say a silencer. That reduces power and accuracy, and this shot was dead-on, with a light enough caliber to make not much more than a small hole. I've seen the kid. He looks like he's sleeping. Only one hole, by the way. The bullet's still in the middle of his brain. Ballistics will say a rifle, autopsy will say death instantaneous. Mr. Holmes, what we got here, in my opinion, is a crack shot with a rifle and a scope."

"The angle?"

"Won't know for sure until the autopsy, but point of entry is behind the right ear. Facing the Padre there, that would mean from the house, terrace, or the trees in that area. The house was swarming with hired help, because food was next on the agenda. But the regular help, who knew the bride, were all allowed to gather on the terrace, looking down on the lawn. That had been arranged by the mistress of the house, so they could witness the wedding. Which made seventeen more observers of the crowd, by the way, although inexperienced ones.

"So a sniper could have been on the roof, in a second-floor window, or in that stand of trees. The only access to the roof is a flight of stairs from the second-floor hallway, and a butler and a maid were sitting there. It was their job to dress the wedding party and they were still there on a break. The windows all give onto the rooms that give onto the hallway. When Delbart went to the roof, he told them to hold still. Nobody came or went. Afterwards he checked all the upstairs rooms. They vouch for each other, so unless they're in on it, and got by the background check, nobody was on the second floor.

"You couldn't hit the kid from the first floor. That leaves only the trees. I don't think anyone could have gotten down from the trees before Hugo and I crossed through there to the gate. On the way back we checked thoroughly. On top of that, the whole place has been manicured clean as a whore's toenails. The grounds were raked and hosed at six A.M. this morning. Except for on the lawn, terrace, and driveway, there isn't the footprint of a hummingbird anywhere on the estate. There's no way you can get out of those trees without leaving one, I'll swear. You'd have to cross almost one hundred yards of raked, soft dirt and flower gardens. If you did, you'd have to arrive either there on the lawn, and you'd show up right in front of the regular staff on the terrace here, who by then had to think something was up because the kid was lying down before his 'I do's,' or you could cross the lawn below the guests. Then you'd come to a sheer cliff that drops onto the rocks in the bay. The estate, between that cliff and the fence, is completely surrounded. Harrington has a net worth equal to Rhode Island, so the place is no stranger to security.

"Which brings up the last thing I can think of: there's a radar scope with a peripheral burglar alarm. It was switched on when the last of the guests arrived. Only the two guys at the gate or somebody with a key to the master panel in the house could override it. Nobody had to, because nobody came late or left early. When the kids getting married are the heirs to a fortune, I guess everybody is very polite."

For the first time Hugo, the second of the trio, spoke up. His eyes sparkled behind thick glasses. His short arms stuck out from a squat body. He enunciated his words crisply and slowly.

"What we got here, in other words," he said, "is a murder that couldn't have happened."

Spencer had followed the descriptions visually and now completed a 360-degree turn which had brought the whole of the grounds on the relevant side of the estate into view. He smiled at Mr. Dihje, who smiled back.

There followed a moment of silence made profound by the natural aura of leadership Spencer Holmes was accorded by the three gumshoes. Eventually he filled it.

"In short," he said, "we have a crime worthy of my attentions. Excellent."

Chapter 8

Introduction to a most eccentric man.

At this juncture our most appropriate line of action might be to examine this curious man Mr. Spencer Holmes. Throughout history, a handful of brilliant men have made the investigation and solution of the most complicated and dastardly of crimes their sole business and preoccupation. Historians interested in this unique specialty will certainly have heard the family name, probably in conjunction with a number of baffling cases which arose in the British Isles between the height of the Victorian Era and the onset of the War to End All Wars. (It was, in fact, a Holmes who first diagnosed that Evil Wind which blew in from the East.) These same admirers might, if their knowledge of the legends which form the reputation of this ascetic man is sufficiently complete, now be drawing close to the conclusion that our man Holmes is somewhat of a poseur, or even a fraud. No evidence arises from reputable circles that the Holmes our present protagonist claims descendance from ever sired a family—ever, in fact, even participated in that human act which results in the birth of progeny. Indeed, a well-known characteristic of the often aloof man was—how to put it gently?—a mild misogyny. His entire life was lived in that comfortable bachelorhood beloved by Englishmen in general (and philologists in particular)—a monastic existence, intellectual, unromantic, unclouded by emotion.

With one exception.

And a notable exception that was: the only antagonist ever to best the enviably successful man. Holmes encountered her in the spring of 1887 in conjunction with a photograph in her possession which he sought on behalf of a client—a monarch in Bohemia attempting to avoid a family scandal. She was dark-haired and handsome, with deep eyes, which could blaze into a man's soul and leave a tattoo there from which he would not

easily be freed. This is precisely what she did in those days
when circumstances in the neighborhood of St. John's Wood
threw them into close proximity for a brief interlude.

Little of this was recorded by the doctor acting at that time
as Holmes's Boswell. For this reason, many devotees of his
biography hasten to the conclusion that little, if anything, resulted from their encounter. This is where they go wrong.

Holmes was a man of unfathomable and inexhaustible sensitivity. Much of this man's notorious arrogance and icy temper-
ament was in fact a defense against the slings and arrows of
emotion from which such a man might suffer. His faithful companion and attending physician knew this well, and by meticulous censorship of his published anecdotes aided him in
defining the limits of a reputation which would otherwise have
suffered from the sniggering of Fleet Street gossips.

What really happened was this: the world's first consulting
detective fell deeply in love.

In failing to record this, his archivist unwittingly laid down a
law which numerous subsequent imitators have rigidly adhered
to, and throughout the twentieth century those men dedicated
to the destruction of evil have been considered immune to blandishments from the fairer sex. Such a reputation has not only
dislodged the effectiveness of whatever line these men wish to
employ when going on the make, but it has given rise to a whiff
of suspicion that the vocation itself promotes impotence. In
fairness to Dr. Watson, who is responsible for this unfortunate
state of affairs, he surely had no idea what havoc he would
wring on the self-esteem of these honorable men.

We might say right now that neither Spencer Holmes nor his
grandfather before him (on his father's side, for it is the direct
paternal lineage to which the grandson claims heir) suffered
from this affliction.

On the 4th of May, in the year of our Lord, 1891, it will be
recalled by Victorian historians, two men were thought to tumble over the Reichenbach Falls near Meiringen, Switzerland.
This was no accident. They were locked in mortal combat and
a fatal conclusion seemed inescapable. Those aware of
Holmes's awesome talents were nevertheless skeptical. Those
believers in the Divinity's inevitable willingness to come down
upon the side of God, Right, and Empire were equally skepti-

cal. Both camps were rewarded. After a silence of nearly three years, the detective surfaced.

It has never been satisfactorily recorded exactly how this restless and resourceful man employed his time during those years. Nor is it possible to do so now. There were rumors of a trip through Tibet. (Spencer Holmes found some evidence of this when he went there on an excursion for precisely that purpose.) It is almost certain that he spent some of his time in London, in disguise, directly under the nose of both friends and enemies, in the pursuit of information that, given his famous profile, would otherwise have been unavailable to him. But for most of those three years, he was in the company of that woman who, four years earlier, had left the fragrance of her delicate perfume floating in the chambers of his heart. The contralto Irene Adler.

His grandfather's biographer left Spencer and the world a facsimile of a letter written to the detective by the New Jersey Prima Donna. A chaste missive whose only hint of deeper meaning is that it begins and ends with the diminutive "My Dear" and includes the cloaked reverence "You took me in completely." Indeed he had. Spencer alone has been left the original letter containing that mysterious innuendo. On its reverse lies a message the good Doctor concealed from his reading public just as the detective had concealed it from the Grand Duke. That message, short as it is, hints at the true story behind the Scandal:

"Guess now who holds thee?"

On reading this, Sherlock Holmes understood immediately that his own emotions had not gone unreflected; for he knew the remainder of the Browning poem.

Irene Adler had been rushed into a marriage which, the very next morning, she came to realize was a terrible error. One that would come to haunt her. The tempestuous young romantic had succumbed, during a lull in her career, to just that sort of dream that nearly wrecked the life of Rose Trelawny, late of the Wells. She had married outside the stage. She had engaged as her life's companion a philistine. A civilian. A lawyer.

Being in large measure a kind woman, Irene at first made the very best of their circumstances together, which began with a Grand Tour that occupied the better part of a year. There followed the hectic business of refurbishing a Great House in Hampstead Heath and a town home in Whitehall. Kindness has its limits, however. The unhappiness which followed her growing boredom with the Hedda Gabler role soon began to infect the ménage à deux. Her wish to return to the stage became a desire, her desire a passion, her passion an obsession. By their third year together she was appearing at the Royal Albert, and by their fourth, these appearances expanded to include the great opera houses of the Continent. By this time the strain on their marriage was considerable. If life upon the wicked stage is an irritant to the bliss of young couples, the road is a catastrophe.

It was precisely at this vulnerable moment that the one man whose romantic image had stayed with her since she had first laid eyes on him, the one man the very thought of whom could set her ivory thighs alight, reappeared on her horizon. At the rear of the Opera House, in fact. In standing room.

The specific circumstances, physical and otherwise, of their relationship need not be exploited here. Suffice it to say he was young and handsome, with a searching curiosity that left no stone, however metaphysical, unturned. Suffice it to say she was a magnificent specimen of womanhood with all the physical yearnings of the creative artist who sings in the upper registers. It is also sufficient, then, to allow the reader to imagine the obvious circumstances which were the result of their constant proximity. Their union explains the link between the man now investigating what surely will become known as the Curious Case of the Interrupted Wedding and the man renowned for the investigation of so many curious cases two generations earlier: a male child.

It was an age when general opinion frowned upon unions unsanctified by the Church. Nevertheless, the iconoclasm of the man we might refer to as Holmes the First precluded their adhering to the conservative morals of the time. At any rate, she had not requested nor been granted a divorce. Mrs. Norton, née Adler, a woman of strong will and indomitable spirit, would not again succumb to the limited charms of a housewife's domain. Nor would she subject her only son to the eccentric and dangerous life-style of an unpredictable man engaged in confidential investigations.

Like a Shakespearean tragedy drawing inevitably to its climax, the Great Liaison drew to its close. He, compelled by his fierce need of purpose, ended the hiatus and returned to London to once again cast a cold shadow over the underworld of the city he loved. She, unwilling to give up the itinerant life, continued the *Wanderjahr* alone. Ever after, they loved in silence, though no less passionately.

The mother, with her entourage, provided adequate supervision for a growing boy. Together they traveled the world. Drawn by the affection the citizens of San Francisco have always held for bohemians in general and the purveyors of classical music in particular, Adler *Mère et Fils* found themselves more than once within the graceful confines of that Athens of the West.

And reaching his majority, when the maternal influence naturally waned, it is no surprise that that same city exercised the seductive charm which defines its worldwide reputation and the young man chose to withdraw from the whirlwind life of the International Artiste, into which he had been adopted, and make his home in the welcoming bosom of the seven golden hills, named for the good Friar, Francis de Azis.

The only remaining explanations for the outre lineage of Spencer Holmes is to say that before long the man (Spencer's father) who landed—educated, talented, and with the persistance of his own father and the beauty of his mother—in the haven of a generous society, fell victim to the same sins of the flesh his forebears had, and in much the same way: Spencer's mother was a girl in the chorus of the early San Francisco Opera.

And with that information safely deposited in the chronicle of history, we had better return to the immediate circumstances before the metropolitan police have bundled the available facts into an incomprehensible hobo's kit.

Chapter 9

*Wherein our detective attempts to pick up the
first thin threads of a tangled skein.*

Except that in this case there were no facts. Or at any rate,
no facts relevant to the principal question that arose with the
unexpected turn in the afternoon's event, i.e., who would do
such a thing?

The police department, under the unfaltering direction of
Chief Kelly, gathered as much evidence as was available. They
photographed. They took statements. They combed areas. They
ordered tests. They even painted in white Day-Glo an outline of
the groom's athletic young form on the Astroturf-covered platform where he had fallen. This gruesome bit of business came
as no surprise to followers of television detectives. It need not
be said that Spencer Holmes gave it only the most cursory
glance during his inspection of the mise-en-scène.

And attention he did give in abundance. After separating
from his comrades, who were obligated to make a complete
report to their head office, he strolled about the grounds, hard
upon the heels of the constabulary. Close observation might
only have distinguished their activities from his by the less intense concentration he focused upon the terrain. While they
peered with vengeance upon the lawn and searched diligently
among the shrubbery, he tended to exhibit the air of a poet
hiking across the moors while preparing a stanza or two. He
was distracted, casual, and brooding. In fact, he appeared more
to be searching the very air itself than much of the terra firma.

Next he made his presence known to Chief Kelly. They chat-
ted briefly, touching slightly on the bizarreness of the event,
and renewing an infrequent but long-term acquaintance. Familiar with almost all the personalities in Bay area police depart-
ments, and their hierarchal positioning, Spencer was not
surprised to see her. The Chief, for her part, covered mixed

feelings with brusque professionalism. While on the one hand she admired his reputation and wanted to see the case solved, on the other she hoped to direct these events to a conclusion which would put her on the fast track where promotion was concerned. She had known immediately when the call came in that the case offered an ambitious and talented chief, stalled midpoint in her career, the opportunity for a higher profile. Like any normal citizen, she hoped to serve both justice and herself. But Spencer could upstage her. They shook hands and parted amid mutual encouragements.

Spencer then meandered through the living room, feigning disinterest, listening as the wedding party gossiped among themselves. To any observer, his posture would have seemed as casual as that of a bon vivant at a formal cocktail party—the kind that turns the rest of us into a jellied mass of insecurity. His first perambulations found him eavesdropping on the conversation of several young ushers and bridesmaids who were animatedly discussing various theories of their own. Among the more interesting remarks he overheard were:

"Suicide is out."

"Harold was not the suicidal type."

"You didn't see his dark side. I was his roommate for two years. The man could be morose, let me tell you."

"He had everything to live for."

"Oh for God's sake, he couldn't have committed suicide. We were all standing right there."

"That's what I said in the first place."

"Well then, it was murder."

"I thought we knew that."

"Who would want to murder Harold?"

"The varsity football coach, for one."

"One little fumble."

"It cost us the division title and Coach his chances for an NFL position."

"That was two seasons ago."

"The Coach has a long memory."

"I think we can eliminate the Coach."

"We can't eliminate anyone. Don't you read detective novels?"

"Who else had a pash for Felicity?"

"Who didn't?"

"Say, you squired her all over town last year, as I recall."

"That's right, Bucky here was heartbroken when she dumped him."

"She didn't dump me. We parted amicably."

"Then what caused you to get drunk, break into the Campanile, scream her name across the campus at three in the morning, and throw up over the side?"

"Boyish enthusiasm. What about you? You took her to the Deke's dance."

"I don't think I could shoot anybody."

"That's right, fencing's your game."

"Maybe he was stabbed?"

"Have you all gone bonkers? We were standing right there. I heard a gunshot just before he collapsed."

"So that's what that was. I thought Harold was passing gas."

"The Case of the Gastric Groom!"

"He did have a pained expression on his face."

"No he didn't. He had a smile on his face. Beatific."

"Happy Harold, finally going to get laid."

"Really. He had just turned to Felicity and was whispering *I love you.* I thought it was very romantic."

"Thank you, Marjorie Morningstar."

Spencer moved on. He came across the mother of the bride, who, with the help of a snifter of brandy supplied to her by the butler, had come awake with a start. She had been brought up to date on the situation, and was sharing a sofa with her daughter. He introduced himself and offered his consolations.

"Holmes? Holmes? I don't think—"

"I have worked for your husband from time to time, Mrs. Harrington. He called me earlier this afternoon."

"Aren't you"—Felicity Harrington looked up through teary eyes—"the private detective?"

"I am. I realize it cannot be of much consolation just now, but I will do my best to effect the arrest of the person who is responsible for your unhappiness."

"Thank you. That is very kind."

"I wonder if I might ask you one or two questions?"

"My daughter really shouldn't be subjected to—"

"It's all right, Mother. Anything we can do to help find poor Harold's murderer."

"Did he have any enemies that you know of?"

"Oh no."

"Anyone who may have been angry that you and he were going to be married? Rejected suitors, for example."

"I don't think so."

"Mr. Holmes," Felicity's mother interjected again. "Felicity has been a most popular girl for some time. There have been scads, simply scads, of young men falling all over themselves for her attentions."

"Mother—"

"Let's not be modest, dear. You are a catch. However, Harold was most loyal. We wanted to see her complete her education, and he waited patiently for her to graduate. She was magna cum laude, did you know? Though I can't for the life of me see what is appealing about the history of landscape architecture. We have gardeners for that sort of thing. And to reach her majority, of course."

"I beg your pardon?"

"Mother means we waited until I was twenty-one. Almost, anyway. I'll be twenty-one tomorrow. Harold asked me some months ago, and we set the date then."

"I see. And you can't imagine that anyone might have begrudged your and Harold's happiness?"

"I'm afraid not, Mr. Holmes."

"I'm going to set a guard on you and the house, Miss Felicity. I'd like to ask you to stay close to home. If you go out, please take the guard with you."

"Whatever is this for?" Mrs. Harrington demanded.

"Her protection, ma'am."

"Why would I need protecting, Mr. Holmes?"

"I don't know that just yet. It may be that you are in no danger at all. But I'd rather not take any chances. If you wouldn't mind."

"Whatever you say."

"Thank you. The Pinkerton detective agency will supply men around the clock. They will try to interfere with your activities as little as possible."

Spencer next drifted to a corner of the room where the

groom's father continued to underscore the hubbub of conversation with his own piano improvisations. (It was not often he was able to tickle the ivories of a genuine Bechstein, and he was not going to miss the opportunity. He had, in any case, the sensitivity to stay in a minor key.) Spencer moved into his line of vision, and spoke over the music.

"You are Harold's father, aren't you? My name is Spencer Holmes."

"Pleased to meet you. Call me Deano. Pull up a bar stool. What can I do for you?"

"Do you know if your son had any enemies?"

"No, but hum a few bars and I'll try to play along. Sorry, couldn't help myself. This is a terrible thing. A terrible thing."

"Did Harold say anything to you about the marriage? Was he worried? Excited? Anything at all?"

"He looked forward to it. He was very happy. I gave him the old man-to-man, of course."

"Well, if you think of anything he might have said about getting married, or if you think of anybody who might have wanted your son killed, please let me know. Here's my card."

"Of course. Anything I can do to help. Anything." Deano started to accompany himself. *"Anything I can do . . ."*

Spencer backed away from the piano. He found Mr. Harrington in conference with a young woman.

"Call the Senator, tell him I have to cancel tomorrow morning. Cancel my flight to New York and postpone the Tuesday Board of Directors meeting. Call the police department first thing every morning and get a complete report. Oh, hello, Spencer. I can't thank you enough for coming."

"Hello, Mr. Harrington. I'm sorry about the occasion."

"Bizarre, isn't it? What kind of a lunatic would shoot a nice kid on his wedding day?"

"I'll try to find out."

"Good. I knew I could count on you. These policemen are interviewing all the guests. Absurd. They're taking fingerprints. What good is that?"

"They are traditionally thorough. You never know where a clue will pop up."

"The trail is getting cold."

"I'm afraid it is already. The murderer is almost positively not one of your guests. Whoever fired that shot is long gone."

"Then how . . . ?"

"That I don't know. But we shall see."

"All right. And anything you need, anything at all, you just call me."

"I will."

Following these interrogatories, Spencer strolled back out onto the terrace, satisfied that he had made at least one significant discovery. As he awaited the appearance of his valued Bunter, he passed ten minutes gazing out past the lawn, admiring myriad pleasure vessels negotiating the white-flecked surface of a gray ocean on a darkening Sunday afternoon.

Chapter 10

In which a supporting character makes several of his own observations.

Sowhat Dihje was as lacking in pedigree as Spencer Holmes was rich in it. He had no idea who his parents were, much less his grandparents. His earliest memories of elders consisted of an eccentric group that varied in number depending on the season. They were a traveling band of entertainers. Actors, comedians, musicians, acrobats, magicians, dancers, all in one. Even faith healers, when necessary. In fact, they were brilliant improvisators, ready to play any part and entertain in any style, as needed. They traveled throughout India, venturing as far as Asia on occasion, in two ancient wagons, each pulled by two immense oxen. They stopped wherever it seemed likely they could gather a crowd, whether in the center of an immense metropolis or at a barren crossroads in the wilds of the countryside. There they plied their trade by presenting a combination burlesque show, commedia dell'arte, magic act, and morality play, the content of which changed regularly, depending on their analysis of audience needs, their current complement of talent, and their own whims. They were paid more often in meals than money, yet they were able to maintain a small communal purse containing a moderate collection of rupees. This was probably due to the fact that several of their number often circulated behind the crowds they gathered and practiced the ancient art of the pickpocket.

As antecedents go, this happy band of players is hardly on a par with the San Francisco social register. Be that as it may, it is among them that Sowhat Dihje spent his entire childhood, and a perfectly happy one it was. Why and how he became attached to this menagerie is lost to history, and certainly lost to him. They are his earliest and only memories. The only things certain are that none of them were his natural parents, and that all of them loved him dearly. They taught him their trade, from aerial somersaults to daredevil yak riding, from flute playing and cobra-mesmerizing to the recitation of ancient Hindu poems, from sleight-of-hand tricks with scarves to the infamous "dip" of the pickpocket. He was an extraordinary and precocious learner, which delighted them. By the age of seven he was participating fully in their daily performances.

In their travels he picked up numerous additional talents as well. He was an enormously inquisitive child. He absorbed a dozen Indian and Asian dialects. He learned to cook in many provincial styles. He mixed with the locals easily, by virtue of his ability to mimic local dialects, customs, and attitudes instantaneously. In fact, one might say he had every character trait, and none, for he was a chameleon, imitating everything and anything of his elders that presented itself.

One day the leader of this unique family came to young Sowhat and told him with great solemnity that he was fired. Not in just those words, perhaps, but the effect was equally as devastating. It had never occurred to Sowhat that he would ever be separated from the only way of life he had ever known. He kept a brave—one might even say inscrutable—face, but inside he was crying.

In fact this wrenching change in the direction of his life had been manipulated by those members of the traveling circus who had his best interests in mind. Perfectly satisfied with their own lot, they nevertheless felt strongly that something better was in store for their young protege, and how he should be set off in pursuit of it had been their secret discussion for some months, ever since his thirteenth birthday. Within a short time, an opportunity presented itself. When the hot winds and dry deserts of the equatorial areas drove them into the cool mountains, their travels led them to encounter a small group of monks, men of sincere mysticism, who were heading for the high mountains of Tibet. Bhutan, to be specific, where several monasteries of great renown were maintained. The monks' high caste and their reputation for learning convinced the players' leader that here was exactly the kind of foster guardianship that Sowhat could benefit from, and a deal was made to turn over the young man to the care of these monks. Thus did he spend almost ten years in the pursuit of a graduate education, Zen style.

He was an apt pupil. He learned and learned and learned. But as the years passed, one thing became apparent to his teachers. In spite of a desire to please, a quick wit, and a flawlessly sincere character, he was unhappy. This fact may never have been apparent to any normal human being, but Sowhat's teachers, attuned to the spirit more than the flesh, saw it at once. They had hoped that in time this would change; they secretly knew it would not. One day, after a decade in their company, Sowhat experienced almost the exact conversation he had had with the leader of that group of traveling entertainers, this time with the wisest of the wise old men he had lived with in the stone city of the monks. He was expelled.

A strange feeling overcame him. While unfathomably sad that he would shortly be separated from his second happy home, where, again, he had assumed he would spend the rest of his days, he felt underneath a great sense of adventure. Unwilling to express this even to his closest confidants, deep down he looked to the future with eager anticipation.

He resumed his days of wandering. His inquisitive nature led him, if not throughout the world, certainly throughout the vast subcontinent, where he happily reviewed all the changes that had overcome that great land since his departure a decade before. And what changes they were. Apparently a man by the name of Mahatma Gandhi had led the Indian people through some sort of revolt. Sowhat had left an India that was under the rule of a strange tribe of white men. He returned to an India that was young, exuberant, spirited, and independent. He meandered slowly across the cities and towns, fields and villages, awed, excited, and inquisitive as always.

In the second year of this third epoch in his satisfying life, Sowhat Dihje met, entirely by chance, a young man from the faraway land of America. How it happened that they spent some days in each other's company, Sowhat does not recall. Indeed, it seemed to have no reason or rhyme. They were simply kindred spirits. Spencer was traveling about, looking for clues to the existence of his ancestors, apparently convinced they had once traversed the Tibetan mountains. In any case, he seemed to need a guide, and Sowhat became that guide, with-

out ever actually applying or being hired for the position.
Within several weeks their collaboration bore some sort of
fruit. That is, Spencer held several conversations with local
wise men and unearthed several documents that supported
whatever thesis he had postulated. By this time it was clear that
the two men could not easily be separated, and Sowhat traveled
on with Spencer Holmes, until he arrived in the port of San
Francisco, eager and inquisitive as ever. And there he has remained to this day.

So Sowhat Dihje was a man of his own inestimable talents. It
was in his character to practice them. Trailing after his employer like that character in the Cervantes novel was not for
him. Immediately upon their arrival on the murder scene, the
two friends—for in addition to their relationship of man and
manservant they harbored a fierce loyalty to and admiration for
each other—separated. Each went after that information which
might be more readily available to him. Mr. Dihje, who had
had the foresight to exchange his traditional Indian garb for a
black-and-white tuxedo circa 1950, promptly circulated among
the hired help. He cozied up to the servants.

He was an observer of keen ability and total recall. His duty,
as he saw it, was to collect as much information as he could
without raising the informants' suspicion that he was in any
way connected with the bureaucracy of the investigation, or
causing apprehension in anyone who might be harboring some
portion of guilt. He emanated cool charm, which assured
housemaids and cooks they could confide in him. He was able
to portray a certain amiable incomprehension customarily seen
in foreigners, which allowed butlers and chauffeurs to feel superior and fed their already considerable braggadocio. Given
these two qualities, there were not many backstairs confidences
which, with patience, he did not share.

It was not, however, in his nature to pursue deductive rea-
soning. Mr. Dihje was a man not of logic but of mysticism, the
result of his childhood comradeship with Himalayan monks.
Logic and mysticism are not comfortable bedfellows. Regarding clues, his lot was merely to collect what information he
could on the principal topic, and package it coherently for his
more conclusion-oriented employer.

When he felt he had used up his welcome, he drifted away as

unobtrusively as he had drifted in, and, spying his sponsor leisurely strolling the terrace, joined him there. On the chance
that the man was indulging in delicate calculations which
might be upset should he be taken by surprise, Mr. Dihje indicated his presence with a small clearing of his throat, then
waited. Spencer recognized this as a sign that Mr. Dihje had
succeeded in collecting the servants' gossip, and opened the
conversation.

"What are they saying, Mr. Dihje?"

Even after some years in this country, Mr. Dihje has a tendency to fracture the English language. We will therefore col-
late the facts he presented in a more convenient form.

1. Both families had sufficient ready cash to insure the future
of any number of footloose young couples. Money, therefore,
was dismissed as a matrimonial motive.

2. No known threats had been made by anyone. This included spurned lovers, social antagonists, and any members of
those radical organizations that seem to think that public and
private displays of accomplishment and stability threaten the
future of the revolution.

3. In the history of the Harringtons at their Belvedere estate,
nothing unsavory had ever transpired. Many of the servants
were especially eager to establish this. (Presumably these sorts
of things tend to reflect badly on them should it be necessary to
seek new positions.)

4. The bride was the apple of her entire family's eye. She had
been adopted as a baby, as Mrs. Harrington had been advised
against becoming pregnant again following two difficult births
that resulted in a pair of strapping boys.

5. The family had welcomed the groom as a harbinger of
closer relations between Harrington Industries and several major banking and investment firms controlled by the boy's immediate family.

6. None of the regular servants had seen anything unusual
prior to the gunshot. Many of them had not quite understood
at first the nature of the disturbance. After the boy had
slumped to the ground, no one had seen anyone leaving the
estate.

7. The temporary servants all knew one another from previous assignments. None were considered blameworthy.

8. The groom's father and mother were an eccentric pair, but not exceptionally so for the wealthier classes.

9. Until someone had taken matters into his or her own hands, the affair had been going smoothly.

10. Preparations for the event had proceeded under the direction of Mrs. Harrington's social secretary. Outside of the numerous hours working out who should sit at whose table, the three months of planning were unremarkable.

After this recitation, which included descriptions of all the help and corroboration regarding their whereabouts at the time of the murder, Mr. Dihje fell silent. The two men—one tall, lean, with a shock of uncontrollable gray hair imparting the only sense of carelessness to otherwise stern, aquiline features, the other short, with deep pools of watery blue eyes set in a fine, delicate, olive face—walked to the living room, where Chief Kelly was overseeing the taking of the statements.

Chapter 11

Wherein our detective swiftly sets further investigative procedures into motion.

Uniformed patrolmen were herding everyone present in and out of a small study off the living quarters, where four male detectives were taking the names and addresses of everyone present. After a brief interview, the guests were encouraged to depart. Kelly was speaking to Harrington. The three Pinkerton men were standing sheepishly by the door. Spencer joined them.

"Gentlemen, what are your orders?"

The three men stared at each other. Once again, the one called Louis took the initiative.

"We were told to stay here and do whatever we could for you."

"Ah, yes. Harrington has probably been in touch with your superiors already. Here is the itinerary then. Hugo, investigate the boy's background, unobtrusively if you can. What he has been up to, especially in the last few weeks. That sort of thing. Perhaps someone wanted him dead."

"Right."

"Louis, we shall need ancestral tables for both the bride and the groom. The bride may be the more difficult; she was an adoptee. It is vital, however. Start with the usual genealogical societies. When you've got that, cross-check it against the list of guests. Perhaps someone wished to prevent this marriage."

"Yes, sir."

Spencer turned to the third operative, a man with the body of a champion power lifter and the demeanor of a Saint Bernard.

"Delbart, remain on the scene. There is good reason to worry about the girl's safety at this point, particularly in the next twenty-four hours. Keep her inside and away from anyone

Harrington doesn't know well. Pull up the moat, so to speak. It shouldn't be too difficult under the circumstances."

Delbart nodded.

"That's all then. Communicate your results to the Pinkerton office. I will call in regularly. We must move swiftly, but with vigilance. There is good reason to assume we may have only experienced the tip of a troublesome iceberg."

Idle chatter was not a part of the Spencer Holmes nature. As he began to quit the scene, however, he could not help but notice the hangdog expressions of the three men. Spencer spoke to them gently.

"Unfortunately, there was no opportunity for you to prevent this tragedy."

Delbart, speaking in a deep voice with a passion which revealed the unhappiness he felt, said, "You know something about this, Mr. Holmes?"

There was more than a little incredulity in the question. Spencer lowered his voice to a confidential tone.

"Well, I know how, of course. But why? That is still unclear. When we know that, we may be able to lay our hands on the culprit. It will not be easy. We are after a daring and reckless criminal, desperate, but with extraordinary resources of nerve and ingenuity. At any rate"—and here Spencer could not help expressing a cliche he treasured—"the game's afoot."

Part II

Chapter 1

A beginning at last.

Inactivity drove Spencer nearly mad. It was three full days before he could take hold of the investigation again, though it was not for lack of effort. A file in Spencer's Macintosh computer was slowly filling up with the facts of the case. These provided considerable nourishment for idle speculation. Information came and was dissected, with Spencer acting the role of spider at the center of his network of contacts. But this was not the sort of activity that a man of action coveted. He yearned for a real break in the case.

It was early Thursday morning, while Spencer awaited breakfast in the nook attached to the kitchen, still in his dressing gown and sipping his Darjeeling, that an event reported in the newspaper gave him cause for action.

"Great Scott!"

Mr. Dihje, unaccustomed to any such outbursts from his employer so early in the morning, knew at once that some vital turn had occurred. He hurried to take his place at the Sleuth's side.

"Read this, Mr. Dihje. Read it aloud, the better to be savored."

He handed over his morning copy of *Vaudeville,* to which he subscribed out of a lifetime's fascination with the performing arts.

Mr. Dihje read:

EXEC OF TOPLESS CLUB
DIES IN FREAK MISHAP
WITH CLAMSHELL, GIRL

Harry Pearl, 40, assistant manager of the Bald Eagle topless club, was crushed to death Sun. nite when a me-

chanical clamshell accidentally closed while he was entangled with a nude woman inside.

The clamshell prop has been used at the club for 20
years as intro shtick for topless dancers.

The Coroner's office

(continued on page 99)

HE DIED HAPPY

(continued from page 1)

speculated Pearl may have been asphyxiated because his
chest was unable to expand enough to breathe. Police
said victim may have accidentally kicked the "close"
button on the shell.

His girlfriend, Jean Darling, 23, sustained only
bruises. She told police she had been drinking heavily
and remembered little until she woke up inside the clam;
she could not explain why she was nude, police said.

Incident occurred at least two hours after club's closing time; Pearl and the girl were found by janitor next
morning, inside the clam. It took fire department rescue
team nearly three hours to free Darling from under victim's body.

Mr. Dihje ceased. There was a fullness in the air, though
neither of the men spoke. Finally Spencer, who was a man
accustomed to filling an inquisitive silence, sketched his
thoughts.

"Don't you see? That very same night. It is the next significant step in the Curious Case of the Disappointed Bride."

"But sire, sir, accidental death in flagrante delicto not unusual in San Francisco. Harrington wedding entirely uncon-
nected. Both undoubtedly most exceptional, but circumstances
at work only coincidental, to be sure."

"Nonsense. There is too much of the inexplicable luggaged
within a single evening. Mr. Dihje, remember this: the unusual
may be coincidental, but the extremely bizarre is never happen-
stance. Come, we must bestir ourselves while the trail is still
warm."

Chapter 2

Featuring an excursion into the city's lower depths.

Moments later the two were sitting on a shoeshine stand across the street from the nightclub known as the Bald Eagle at the triangular intersection of lower Broadway, Grant Avenue, and Columbus. Spencer wore his customary working clothes—tan safari jacket and pants and a desert hat—and Mr. Dihje wore loose harem pants and a richly brocaded jacket.

Spencer lowered a newspaper, and they cautiously surveyed the scene. The street, illuminated not by its customarily flattering neon but by the truer light of a pink dawn rising over the financial towers to the southeast, appeared dismal. Trash littered the sidewalks. Denizens of the murky topless strip had not yet begun to stir. Beneath our duo, a woman approaching fifty, with two inches of black roots supporting orange hair, worked efficiently over Spencer's handmade brogans. Her pendulous, uncovered breasts swung rhythmically to and fro and the cold air raised little dots of protest over the broad mesas of her glutei maximi, which were neatly divided by a thin length of green glitter. A birthmark flashing in and out of view under her left teat fascinated Mr. Dihje, but Spencer kept his eye firmly on the pleasure palace across the street.

Soon a man holding his toupee against the wind came up the street and entered the foyer of the nightclub. He unlocked the door and disappeared between floor-to-ceiling signs reading "NAKED LOVE ACTS."

Spencer counted thirty seconds, tipped the footwear specialist, and led the way across the broad avenue to the concrete venue of voyeurism. He rapped lightly at the door. It creaked open and the man's sour face peeked out.

"We're closed."

"I can see that, my good man."

"Come back after twelve."

"I think not. I mean this as no criticism of the talent, but we're not interested in the entertainment exactly. We'd like to speak with you."

"Who the fuck are you?"

"My name is Holmes. This is Mr. Dihje. The little cylinder he holds in his hand is employed for the purpose of propelling a small dart into the epidermis. This has the effect of putting a Bengal tiger weighing 350 pounds to sleep instantaneously. They have been known to sleep for forty-eight hours. I have seen it myself. How much do you weigh, Mr. . . . I'm afraid I didn't get your name?"

"What the fuck is going on here?"

"Why don't we carry this discussion on in more privacy? We'd like very much to make certain observations of the interior decor of this establishment."

"Is this a holdup? You're outta your mind. You got any idea who owns this place?"

"Indeed I do. We have exchanged favors from time to time. However, there was no time to communicate with him, and we took the chance someone might be at home. I'm sorry for this little persuasion, but we are prepared to see that the unexpected does not hinder our investigation. That would, unfortunately, include you."

Mr. Dihje pushed forward, keeping the bamboo instrument level with the fleshy paunch that overhung the man's cowboy belt buckle. The man walked backward until the three were inside the club. The room was stale with the permanent smell of dried liquor and cigarette smoke. Chairs were upended and set upon small circular tables. A long bar against the wall was littered with crumpled cocktail napkins, and the entire room was bathed in a sickly fluorescent light. Not at all the ambience of the erotic pleasure palace that was advertised. Mr. Dihje put away his blowgun, but stood uncomfortably close to, and kept his eyes fastened intently upon, the manager. It had the effect of putting the man into a cold sweat.

"Say, is this Chink safe?"

"He is exceptionally capable of protecting himself, yes."

"I mean, am I safe from him? Is he going to do something?"

"Oh. Well, that depends on your willingness to cooperate. We need certain information, and a chance to look around. Also, make no sudden moves, please. We wouldn't want a misunderstanding to arise. Now. Is this the clam which crushed the life out of Mr. Pearl last Sunday night?"

"Huh? Oh, yeah, yeah. He was my assistant manager."

"Exactly how was he found?"

"The janitor opened up and noticed the girl's leg sticking out. He called me. I called the police. They called the fire department."

"To release the girl?"

"Yeah. She was caught inside the clam with him. The clam was closed, see, not open. It closes up hydraulically and there's only room inside for one person. It rises up from the basement through a hole in the stage. The dressing room is down there."

"How does it operate?"

"Uh, there's a switch right on the side. The girls work it themselves."

"There are no other controls?"

"No. Say, are you a policeman? That's impossible."

"I am an interested party."

"Holmes. I heard that name before."

"Quite possibly. What time did this take place?"

"After they closed up. Two a.m. in this town."

"And there was no one else present?"

"No, I guess not."

"Was the front door locked from the inside?"

"Yeah, sure. The janitor had to open it like always. I was surprised, I tell you."

"May I take it that both parties were in dishabille?"

"Take it what?"

"Were they undressed? Naked?"

"Oh, sure, sure. You know anybody who does it with their clothes on?"

"Eskimos sometimes. I'll ask the questions, however. Here is a piece of paper. Write down the full name and address of the girl."

"I gotta go behind the bar for my address book."

"All right."

The manager moved behind the counter. Mr. Dihje followed two steps behind.

While he did this, Spencer moved to the exotic prop and examined it minutely. Then, in complete disregard for the austerity he usually projected, he climbed on the velvet bed inside and lay on his back.

"Which way were they facing when you found them?"

"The other way. He was on top. You know."

"Yes. The missionary."

At this point Spencer not only energetically scooted 180 degrees, but he began wiggling immodestly and waving his hands overhead in a display that surely must have startled even the unfazeable Mr. Dihje. If it did, however, he gave no sign. Then, abruptly, the velvet-lined clam closed and descended through a trapdoor in the stage floor. The assistant manager and Mr. Dihje stared at the space where the imitation crustacean had been. A moment later it reappeared and opened. Spencer stepped out nonchalantly. He spoke casually into the startled face of the manager.

"There must be an alternate entrance?"

"There's a back door."

"Where?"

"Through that opening beyond the stage."

"And it was secured when you arrived that morning?"

"Yeah."

Spencer then disappeared through the opening. For some minutes the club was quiet. The manager turned to Mr. Dihje and smiled. Mr. Dihje nodded. Together they waited. As suddenly as he had disappeared, Spencer returned. There was in his eyes the subtle but unmistakable look of success.

"That's all, I think. You have been most helpful." Picking up the slip of paper on the bar, he went toward the door. Mr. Dihje followed. "These are correct, I hope. Otherwise I shall be most aggravated."

"The addresses are correct. But I can't vouch for the girl still being there. She quit the next day."

"Really? I should have guessed. We must hurry."

"Holmes . . . ? Holmes . . . ? There's a Sherlock Holmes. You don't think you're him, do you?"

"Of course not."

"He ain't real."

"I'm his grandson."

"Yeah? Listen, there's an Emperor in this town, you oughta know. His name's Norton. Why don't you two have a talk? You'd have a lot in common . . ."

But Spencer and Mr. Dihje were out the door before the manager had finished.

Chapter 3

A serendipitous encounter with a skittery ecdysiast.

In a narrow alley running alongside a white building behind the Broadway area that Spencer and Mr. Dihje had hurried to, they stood outside a weathered door contemplating a line of buttons. Most of them bore no identification, and this included number seven, the one they were seeking. Spencer spoke.

"We don't want to flush the rabbit. You go up the fire escape. I'll knock at the front door directly. No, wait a moment—the sight of you at a rear window might have an upsetting effect on the young lady. I'll take the fire escape."

In a moment the two men were in place. Mr. Dihje rang the bell. Rewarding the preparations of Spencer, the girl immediately appeared, in some haste and with a suitcase in her arms, at the kitchen window, where she was startled by the smiling visage of her pursuer.

"Good afternoon. Miss Darling, I presume. Allow me to introduce myself. My name is Holmes, Spencer Holmes. The man at the front door is my assistant." Spencer stepped through the window into the kitchen. "Kindly let him join us, if you wouldn't mind."

The girl stood speechless.

"Ah, never mind, here he is now. Picking locks is a bit of a hobby with him. I'm sure no damage has been done. Perhaps we would be more comfortable in your dayroom, yes? In here, I think."

Spencer led her gently to a threadbare couch and she sat down automatically, still silent, and still clutching the suitcase.

"We mean you no harm. I can understand your trepidation. If I might be so crude, you are scared witless. Is this correct?"

Jean Darling was statuesque and well-endowed, as her chosen profession required, but slumped over in a round-shouldered posture that lacked confidence. She tugged at the soft black hair on her shoulders. She adjusted the suitcase on her lap. Her interlocutor waited patiently. Finally he spoke.

"Why, I wonder, didn't you leave town three days ago?"

The girl adjusted the suitcase again. She felt for the top button on a faded cotton blouse. At last she spoke.

"I had no place to go."

"I see. And now . . . ?"

"I got a chance for a job in Reno."

"A fresh start. Good. Well, it's an ill wind, as they say. We wish you the best of luck. Could you answer a few questions before your departure?"

"I didn't see anything, I swear."

"No, I wouldn't have thought so. A good thing, too, as our man seems to be both ruthless and fastidious. However, if you would describe the scene, as it were, we would be grateful."

"I . . . we . . . were on the velvet bed in the clam. I guess the thing got switched on by accident. Next thing I knew—"

"No, Miss Darling, it won't do. See here, we are neither reporters, with their traditional disregard for accuracy, nor the metropolitan forces, anxious to close a case quickly. Explanations need a little more substance with us. We have some information already, you see."

"I didn't kill him! I didn't touch the damn switch!"

"I know that. You couldn't have. I tried it myself from your, um, position, and it was extremely difficult. But, of course, that eliminates accident as well. And my arms are longer than yours. The electrical system, by the way, was intact. No, there was a third party present, wasn't there? This is confirmed by the fact that the rear door had been jimmied. I found evidence to that effect just now. You may be relieved to find out that we therefore consider your conspiracy in the matter unlikely. You would have simply let him in. Now. What precisely, exactly, really, happened?"

The girl's voice was small when at last she spoke.

"Could I have a drink of water?"

"Certainly."

This attended to by the solicitous Mr. Dihje, the girl became somewhat less ill at ease. She still clutched the suitcase tightly, however.

"Well, we were in the clam. On the velvet. Oh, I told you that. But the top was up. Anyway, suddenly everything went dark."

"You were knocked unconscious?"

"Naw. Someone blindfolded me. I thought it was Harry at first. He was always doing kinky things. It was my own G-string, and the sequins scratched my eyes."

"A brilliant improvisator, our man," Spencer muttered in an aside to Mr. Dihje, then returned to Miss Darling. "Please continue."

"Well, then Harry was struggling like mad. I could feel him. He's not usually that wild, if you know what I mean. The next thing you know, the damn clam's closing up. I started to scream, but somebody put their hand over my mouth. I was really scared. There was some kind of fight going on, and Harry was swearing like mad. All of a sudden we were locked inside. I was, you know, still underneath. And then Harry wasn't moving and the other man was gone. It took a few minutes to get the blindfold off, because Harry was on my arm. I couldn't reach the switch, and I couldn't get out from under Harry. I yelled a little while, then I just waited. It seemed like a long time went by. Harry was unconscious. I didn't know he was dead. Anyway, next thing I hear, Benny, that's the day manager, he's yelling his head off. The fire department's getting me out. You ever get dressed in front of a dozen firemen?"

"I don't believe so."

"Well, it was humiliating, I can tell you."

"You gave your notice the next night?"

"I'm not hanging around here. People might think I know something. I don't. Harry was a sweet guy, but how do I know what he was into? Maybe his wife killed him. Maybe she'll kill me."

"Harry was married?"

"Yeah."

"Do you know if he had any children?"

"No, not yet. Not now, either."

"Harry Pearl, the end of a line."

"What?"

"Sorry. I was talking to myself."

She looked at Spencer with apprehension.

"There is one more thing. This photograph"—Spencer nodded to a frame on the coffee table—"is of Mr. Pearl, I assume? You're leaving it behind?"

"Well, let bygones be bygones, I always say."

"Yes. I'll take it, then, if you don't mind. It may prove useful."

The girl shrugged. After Spencer had picked up the picture and examined it for a moment, she spoke again.

"There's a bus to Reno at noon."

"Oh, yes, certainly," Spencer responded.

"I can go?"

"I suggest it. There are evil forces at work here."

"There's a bunch of freako nutcakes running around this city."

"Infinitely better put. Allow us to escort you to the bus station. We have delayed you, and you are owed at least that courtesy."

The trio, occasioning an ample share of curious glances, walked the several blocks to the Greyhound station side by side by side. There they parted, with salutations.

Chapter 4

Wherein modern technology demonstrates an efficiency at least equal to the Baker Street Irregulars.

At the nearest phone booth, Spencer punched in his own telephone number, and heard his own voice.

"You have reached Spencer Holmes and Sowhat Dihje. We are otherwise engaged. There will be a beep tone, after which leave your name, number, and needs. Thank you."

After the beep, Spencer whistled a perfect fifth into the mouthpiece. He was answered by the whirring of a tape, several clicks, and a message.

"Mr. Holmes? This is Hugo. We've tracked down the adoption agency of the girl. Harrington picked her up at the Mt. Sinai hospital, and the hospital made arrangements with the Sisters of Mercy Orphanage on California Street, north of Van Ness. I went over there but without a court order I couldn't get a look at the file. What do you want me to do next? I'll be at the Pinkerton office."

There was another beep.

"Hello, this is the Gotham Book Mart calling. We've obtained a first edition of Grossett's *Nineteenth Century Poisons.* Just came in from London. Fair condition, no dustcover. The price is forty dollars. We'll hold it until we hear from you."

Another beep. This time an excited, high-pitched voice.

"Shandi Bakshee, wonder no lotso iskent. Effem mondu letshaso can sen dunher. Renless bolu ekstine lendal. Effendi."

There were then two quick beeps in succession, and another whirring of the tape. Spencer replaced the receiver and set off with Mr. Dihje at his side.

"Excellent. Our book dealers have located a copy of the Grossett. I'm convinced it will confirm my suspicion in the

Robbins murder. The widow will undoubtedly confess when we confront her with our superior knowledge. I wonder how she got hold of *nurmanium serum*? Ah well, the ingenuity of women, eh?"

These remarks drew Mr. Dihje's attention to a case that had been pending for some time. The widow in question was a blonde in her early twenties with a murky past whose attractions had caused one of San Francisco's elder statesmen to divorce his wife and change his will, shortly after which his health deteriorated rapidly, until he was found to be non compos mentis. After a brief competency hearing, the events passed from the front page. When Spencer was approached by the husband's first wife with the information that the doctor who had initiated the legal proceedings and who represented the blonde's family was the brother of the blonde, he had undertaken a circumspect investigation.

"Oh, by the way," Spencer went on. "Your lodge meeting for this evening has been postponed. Either that, or your cousin is arriving Tuesday on the Queen Isadore. I'm afraid I'm still a bit rusty on the Hindu dialect."

Just then they heard the musical clang-clang that harbingered their transportation.

"Here's the cable; we're off to make a surreptitious visit to some sisters of the cloth."

They stepped onto the runner and rode outside the polished-wood cable car up the steep hill. Spencer stood lightly on the step, both hands in his pockets, and leaned against the car's front wall.

Mr. Dihje, among whose childish delights was riding the cable, held on to his pole and leaned out, smiling like a dog in the wind. Unable to recall any relatives who could be expected to arrive in the civilized world on Tuesday, he was satisfied that he was released from his obligations for the evening.

Chapter 5

A justified intrusion on the privacy of nuns.

Spencer Holmes was a man unwilling to manhandle a nun, so the two men waited patiently across the street from the Sisters of Mercy Orphanage until the yard alongside suddenly filled up with little girls in starched white blouses and gray plaid skirts, herded by a number of full-sized penguins. Spencer and Mr. Dihje then walked casually to the front of the building until they were out of sight of the yard, sprinted up the stairs, and quickly located a door marked "OFFICE." Mr. Dihje opened the door and they slipped within the inner sanctum, where they were momentarily stymied. A bank of files appeared to be organized by date. Spencer, with the caution of the thoughtful, paused.

"Dates. Let me see. Of course, the date of the adoption. They must be cross-referenced somewhere. Never mind, we know when she was placed. At birth. That would be 1967. Here it is."

He pulled open a drawer marked 1967. It contained a number of folders. Each was sealed shut with wax and an imprint.

"Damn! They're really particular about this stuff, I say. Well, no matter, we've broken the law before. An honest man must make his own decisions between right and wrong; the girl could be in danger still, and the law would grind exceedingly fine and slowly on a request of this nature."

But Mr. Dihje, who came from a country with a long, rich history of civil disobedience, had already extracted half the files and placed them on a desk. He was busily involved making a neat slit between the paper and the wax with a thin instrument that had appeared suddenly from the folds of his tunic. As each folder was slit open, he placed it in a neat pile before his partner in crime.

Spencer withdrew the papers that had been secured in the first envelope and read through them quickly.

"Here it is. Halfway down the second page. 'Adopters.' That should read 'Harrington' on one of these. Not this one, I'm afraid. Well, here we go."

For the next ten minutes the two men worked swiftly side by side and resembled nothing so much as a well-oiled machine, Mr. Dihje making a swift pass at the top envelope, Spencer withdrawing the papers, quickly shifting the top page, then replacing them.

"No . . . no . . . no . . . no . . ."

The pile before the diligent Dihje was almost diminished to nothing when Spencer raised his voice ever so slightly.

"Eureka."

With that one word, Mr. Dihje looked at his leader, saw the light of confidence in his eyes, and moved from Spencer's left to his right side. Using a small brass lighter, Mr. Dihje now passed a flame briefly under the wax and pressed it to the envelopes, resealing each of the files. At the same time, Spencer had spread four pages of the document he wanted on the desk directly under the lamp, and was in the process of photographing each piece with a tiny Leica. Between the third and fourth clicks of the shutter, conversation could be heard approaching. Both men ceased their actions immediately and looked at the door.

It was Spencer who formulated a rear-guard action. He leaped silently to the door and slid the bolt. Then he returned to the desk, clicked off one last frame, and replaced the documents in the envelope. Going to the only window, he slid the sash upwards and looked out, where he was pleasantly surprised to see a large, overflowing dumpster almost directly below the window, not more than twelve feet away.

"Are you familiar with *Butch Cassidy and the Sundance Kid,* Mr. Dihje?"

Mr. Dihje, who had resealed all of the files and was now replacing them in the cabinet, said something in his native language which, roughly translated, bore upon the shallowness of American films. Then he appeared at Spencer's side.

"Never mind. We shan't have much difficulty. On your mark, get set, go . . ."

And with that expression, the two men, side by side on the windowsill, launched themselves into the air. The full gainer with which Mr. Dihje completed the atmospheric part of the maneuver startled Spencer, who chalked it up to the child's play of which his friend was so fond. In any case, they landed safely.

Over their heads, a rattling of the door commenced. A conversation concerning the ineptitude of certain junior members of the staff was heating up, and resulted in a Mr. Gonzalez, the building's engineer, being sent for. But by the time the door was unlocked, the pair of intrepid burglars had brushed off an accumulation of odiferous debris, beat it up the alley, and caught a trolley home.

Chapter 6

Linking the investigations of the previous chapter with those of the next.

We now wait patiently in the book-lined library on the second floor of the habitat of Spencer Holmes and Sowhat Dihje. This room contains several comfortable leather armchairs flanking a fireplace, two window seats in tall windows facing the bay, and an ornate partners desk. The walls are lined with a large collection of volumes, an eclectic assortment with a specialty in crime. A bibliophile, Spencer Holmes has a number of prize possessions. (Not the least of which is a near-complete collection of *Strand* magazines. Eat your heart out.) First editions do not figure prominently in his extensive library, however. It is the content rather than the veneer of books he loves. Used hardbounds are, in fact, his favorite quarry, preferably long out of print and unavailable in mall bookstores.

Mr. Dihje also waits patiently. He is not immune to the enchantment of books, and his own interests range from detective stories featuring America in the 1940's—upon which he practices his English—to cookbooks, his own particular specialty. The cornucopian abundance of international staples available in San Francisco actually initiated this avocation, to the delight of his sponsor, and just now he uses the time to research the Southern approach to a pheasant he intends to prepare for this evening's repast. In circumstances like these, Spencer has often been known to abandon his usual schedule without notice, and Mr. Dihje would hate to lose a bird he had imported all the way from North Carolina.

A few minutes pass in silence, and then a bookcase we might have assumed was permanently attached to the wall swings open and Spencer emerges from his photographic darkroom. He sits at the desk opposite Mr. Dihje and reads over the four large photographs. Then he recapitulates aloud.

"The bride's last name was Bernstein before it was legally changed to Harrington. She doesn't know it herself, of course. It was recorded on her birth certificate by her natural mother. She was put up for adoption immediately and twenty-four hours later she was welcomed into the lap of luxury by the Harringtons. A lucky little girl. And we're graced with a bit of luck ourselves. The mother's name was Sarah Bernstein, and here's an address. Something funny about it, I can't quite put my finger on why. No father recorded. Mark my words, there is a clue here, and it will be providential of us to follow it. Let's take the automobile; we may have a need to impress."

Chapter 7

A visit to one of San Francisco's finest old homes.

Spencer's father—that is, the man we might refer to as Holmes the Second—had inherited a brilliant gift of deduction from his father, and had applied it to the trading of stocks in the marketplace. As a result he had amassed, in no particular order, a fortune, a good deal of San Francisco real estate, an ulcer, a tendency to put on weight, and a white 1947 Silver Wraith Sedanca-de-Ville with gold-plated appointments where lesser mortals made do with chrome. It was this latter curiosity which Spencer Holmes had referred to obliquely as impressive. He had dubbed it, appropriately, The Legacy. He now piloted the craft adroitly through the narrow, winding San Francisco streets. It was Mr. Dihje's joy to sit beside him, surrounded by an estimable objet d'art. Though you might scoff at the naiveté of a man who would risk such a prized craft on narrow, potholed streets, of late crowded with mad, myopic, Oriental drivers, you would be mistaken. There is a universal tendency to give physical space to an object of awe, and the true luxury vehicle is always given a wide berth, just as are the truly insane. There is also an unspoken understanding among traffic officers that the man who arrives in such a car is on business, the importance of which greatly exceeds the need to observe parking regulations. For these reasons, Spencer arrived safely and steered his vehicle directly alongside a bright red curb, where he left Mr. Dihje in occupancy. Mr. Dihje fished a colorful paperback detective novel out of the glove compartment, and settled down to await Spencer's return. Meanwhile, Spencer approached a large Victorian house, and knew immediately why the address had lodged itself in his mind.

He was standing in front of what had been for thirty years a house of ill repute, a direct lineal descendant of the notorious

Sally Stanford mansion. Sally herself had gone on to other pursuits, including a successful stint in politics (which after all was not such a change in style), but other girls with managerial talents had replaced her, and the bordellos of San Francisco had enjoyed an unbroken run of success. The building Spencer surveyed housed one of the finest.

Discretion had always been an attribute of the Holmes family. This reputation made him welcome where many in his profession were not. More than one of the half a dozen ladies present (for it was midafternoon and the full shift was not yet employed) had made Spencer's acquaintance in his professional capacity, though not, we hasten to add, in theirs.

The Madame herself was delighted to see him, and shortly the two were in conference in a rear apartment that reflected the owner's attachment to the understated elegance of art deco. The discussion proceeded smoothly. Both the seventy-year-old Grande Dame and her questioner were at the very pinnacles of their respective professions, and a mutual admiration bound them together.

After serving an aged Kentucky bourbon in crystal glasses, the Botticellian woman lowered herself into an armchair and gathered a fox boa around her, allowing it to drap over her ample bosom. As she spoke, she fluffed it gently.

"How," she asked in a soft baritone voice, "may I help you, Spencer?"

Spencer came directly to the point, and the woman answered his question with a story fairly bursting with relevancies.

"A darling girl, Sarah. I hated to lose her. Eighteen years old with the face of a fourteen-year-old. You can imagine how valuable the combination is in my business, Mr. Holmes." Here the Madame wistfully ran her hand along the gluteal fold of a nude bronze dancer at her side. "Yes, she had only been here for a little over a year when she came to me with the proposition. Of course, I advised her to take it. I wouldn't stand in the way of the happiness of any of my girls."

The Madame blushed coyly, fluttered enormous eyelids over the edge of her tumbler, and lowered her voice.

"And of course there was a substantial fee involved. The men were quite aboveboard. Real proper gentlemen, you might say."

"Exactly what was the nature of this proposition, my dear lady?"

"A private one, you might say. The five men were regulars here in the early sixties. They were all at that stage in their careers when the office no longer required their complete attention, and they often had time on their hands. They had all made a bundle, if I might be vulgar for a moment. The sixties, you remember, offered a great deal of competition to my establishment. Too many young girls did not fully understand the value of their gifts. My younger clientele began to feel they shouldn't have to pay for their pleasures. Thank goodness that was all a passing fad. The older men, on the other hand, continued their customary ways.

"Anyway, these five men all became very fond of young Sarah. After a while, they wouldn't go to anyone else. This is an occupational hazard in my business. One naturally tries to encourage a less personal approach. Otherwise it can become difficult to gratify their needs, and that, after all, is the service upon which our profession rests.

"Well, when they came to me and offered to purchase an exclusive on her services, I could not refuse. Miss Bernstein was an independent contractor, free to come and go as she pleased. I didn't tell the men that, of course. They were under certain illusions, and we made a satisfactory arrangement."

Spencer attempted to move her story along.

"What, precisely, was this arrangement?"

"They moved her into a small home of her own. Apparently they were satisfied to share visits on a weekly basis. I believe, in fact, they were known to her as much by their nicknames—Mr. Monday, Mr. Tuesday, etc.—as they were by their Christian names. They had families of their own, and this left Sarah free on the weekends. I believe she became quite an accomplished tennis player. I wonder if she still plays."

There was a danger that the woman would slip too firmly into the past, and Spencer rushed to head it off.

"This is rather important, madam. Particularly to Ms. Bernstein, I believe. Do you know where I can find her now?"

"Oh, yes. We keep in touch with Christmas cards and birthday greetings. She's one of my greatest successes. I tell all the girls when they come to me: if you work hard, you'll be rewarded. She's in the same lovely home her five gentleman gave to her. It's a lovely house in the hills above Sausalito. Designed by Stanford White. I believe he had built the house some years before with a similar purpose in mind. Stanny was cut from the same cloth, you know, a real Victorian gentleman."

In an attempt to avoid the recollections of an even more ancient era, in which he would have been fascinated were it not for a growing feeling of urgency, Spencer stood up.

"This has been exceedingly generous of you, my good lady. The information will serve to avert unpleasant circumstances for Ms. Bernstein. Now, if I could just trouble you for the address?"

This formality was dispensed with, and Spencer returned to the street clutching a leaf of pink stationery that gave off the subtle aroma of *White Shoulders*. He slipped behind the wheel of the automobile, put it in gear, and eased back into the traffic, heading for the Golden Gate Bridge.

He glanced at the cover of the paperback his friend was reading. He could not resist revealing his extensive knowledge of the literature of crime. It was the one aspect of his character that could be exceedingly annoying.

"I think you'll find it was the attorney. He swam from the ship to the beach and back again before the boat docked."

Mr. Dihje looked up startled. He thumbed through to the end of *The House Without a Key,* which he had been reading avidly, scanned a paragraph, frowned, and replaced the paperback in the glove compartment. In silent dignity the two men cruised high above the turbulent waters of the Pacific Ocean, each mulling over the complex plot of a diabolical scheme.

Chapter 8

Wherein the ancestry of the bride proves to be a useful revelation.

In Sausalito, Spencer piloted the stately craft along a boulevard choked with tourists. On their right, houseboats of all shapes and sizes floated serenely on the bay. On their left, leather bags and chic cotton dresses crowded every window.

They quit the boulevard and climbed laboriously into the hills. The large automobile was forced to a crawl in the twisting streets. They were sporadically rewarded with a glimpse of the broad blue bay and the skyline of the city beyond. They wound their way past shingled condominiums and Cape Cod cottages. At last they turned steeply up and onto Cloud View Drive.

Mr. Dihje kept a sharp eye on the mailboxes. Arriving at the number they sought, Spencer steered the car alongside a grove of pine, where a narrow path lined with wisteria disappeared through the trees.

The two men got out of the car and picked their way through the undergrowth until they came to a carved door, on either side of which were frosted-glass windows with designs of rollicking nymphets. A wrought-iron handle projected from the center panel. In the quiet of the hills, birds sang their melodies of courtship. The wind rolled pine cones along the path. Spencer depressed the bell and a faint chime reverberated within. Presently soft footsteps could be heard approaching, and the door swung open.

Both Spencer and Mr. Dihje were blithely unaware of the startling effect they tended to create, especially as they stood side by side. Spencer was tall and angular with exceptionally sharp features and unruly gray hair. Mr. Dihje, short and stocky and favoring Eastern dress, looked both childlike and sinister, a combination only made possible by his mixed bloodlines. The middle-aged woman who swung open the heavy door waited with patience for the pair to explain themselves.

"How do you do? I am Spencer Holmes of San Francisco. This is Mr. Sowhat Dihje. You, I can see at a glance, are Sarah Bernstein. Your daughter bears a remarkable resemblance, which may I say is all to her advantage. Which day of the week was it that contributed such complimentary features, if I may be so bold?"

Now at last the woman was startled. However, good breeding told, and she confined herself to a widening of the eyes. This only enhanced the innocent look that her original benefactors had found so beguiling. After a very long moment, Spencer continued.

"I am correct in assuming that your domestic arrangements resulted in the birth of a daughter you named, presciently, Felicity, am I not?"

There was another silence. Apparently Ms. Bernstein had not yet overcome her first shock.

"We are not here to reprimand you for your choice of vocation, or what I assume to be the unexpected result. We merely need to ascertain some facts which could benefit us in an investigation that might bear directly on the safety of your daughter."

"I have no idea what you are talking about."

"Ms. Bernstein, that attitude will only serve to—"

"I mean to say I don't think I can help you. She was adopted out of the hospital the day she was born. Arrangements had been made beforehand."

"Would you mind if we discussed this in more detail?"

Sarah Bernstein eyed them warily. She was an attractive, middle-aged woman with short-cropped, light brown hair and a slim figure. She had the poise of a woman who didn't mind listening to a used-car salesman's spiel, but in the end was not going to buy a car she didn't want. Spencer and Mr. Dihje waited uneasily. At last she placed her hand lightly on the doorknob and swung it wider.

"Why don't you come inside?"

"Thank you."

She ushered them into a foyer that reflected the rich wood

and forest green surrounding its entrance. The sun fell through a skylight, highlighting numerous plants along the wall.

"You'll have to excuse me, I've just come in from riding in Golden Gate Park." Spencer noticed her boots and jodhpurs for the first time as she led them down a few steps and into the living room. She invited them to sit on couches flanking a stone fireplace.

Windows dominated the living area, and beyond it the Bay spread out at their feet. Gray clouds wheeled across the sky. Nearly the whole of the Bay's civilization was visible in one form or another, from the great shipping barges to the small pleasure craft, the automobiles snaking along the endless highways, the tourists scurrying along the quaint streets. Spencer, who had an ardent interest in what he often referred to as the Big Picture, could appreciate such a panoramic view. He complimented her on the house. She smiled, but remained noncommittal.

"This is, may I assume, the original domicile which served your arrangement with your five sponsors?"

"Yes, it is."

"I should perhaps say that I am an acquaintance of your first employer. I have just had a most satisfying visit with her. I understand how you first came here. As the men would now be in their eighties, may I ask if the arrangement still exists?"

"They're all deceased. The last one died seven years ago. But I hadn't seen him in ten. He was ill and his family kept him at home."

"Which one fathered the child?"

Ms. Bernstein looked into the fireplace, where a few dull embers glowed from an earlier blaze. She spoke quietly.

"I don't know."

"Ms. Bernstein, this could be a matter of some importance, and I assure you it is not our intention to illuminate your past against your wishes."

"I'm sorry. I really don't know. Look, Mr. . . . Holmes, is it? Mr. Holmes, perhaps you have some idea that a woman always knows who the father of her baby is. A woman's intuition? I'm afraid that's an old wives' tale. Those men were all my lovers. The baby was conceived during a week in which all five came to visit me on their appointed evening. All of them had children with their wives at one time or another; any of them were capable of fathering a child. When I found out I was pregnant, I was scared. It was some time ago and abortion was illegal. I was afraid they would desert me. Obviously I had to tell them. As it turned out, they were extremely kind, and made all the arrangements for my care and the delivery of the baby. I arranged for the adoption. I was very young and a nun at the hospital who knew I was unmarried told me I ought to place the child somewhere else for its own good. So that's what I did. The nun promised me they would find a good home, and I came back here and continued my own life. In those days it simply wasn't thought of to raise a child alone. Also, I didn't want her to be . . . confused about her father."

This narration seemed to have a profound effect on Spencer. He stared out the window at an increasingly gray sky. His own brow fairly clouded over. He didn't speak, but his face gave away the fact that he was already calculating the effect of the story on his case. Presumably the tale had the same effect on his inexpressive sidekick, whose emotional waters ran deep, if silent. It was the woman who broke the silence.

"Is she in some kind of trouble? I have money. I would be glad to help."

"No, she is not in any difficulty. Not, at any rate, the kind that money could solve. You know nothing about her present circumstances?"

There was an infinitesimal pause, upon which Spencer remarked silently. Then she said, "No, nothing."

"She was adopted by a wealthy family and has had, as far as I can discern, a satisfying childhood. She has just reached her majority, as you must know. But she was engaged to be married and her fiancé met with tragic circumstances. We are attempting to get to the bottom of those circumstances. It may have no bearing on your daughter, but I have an instinct that it does and my instincts, if I may brag momentarily, are formidable. If the fathers are all deceased, I believe it would not be breaking a confidence if you could sketch brief biographies for us. I take it they were men of considerable resources and it would help immensely to have a complete picture."

Sarah Bernstein appeared to consider this request for a moment, during which Spencer and Mr. Dihje waited respectfully. Finally she stood up, smiled courteously, and said to them, "All right. Follow me."

Chapter 9

In which Spencer and Mr. Dihje follow Sarah Bernstein into the past.

The three of them stood before a rolltop desk in Sarah Bernstein's den. On the wall just above the desk hung a series of framed photographs of men in their sixties, each with their arm around a younger version of Sarah. She was fair-haired and blue-eyed, with an open and eager smile. A girl just out of her teen years, as if posing with her proud father. Except that there were five proud fathers.

"Here they are," Sarah said. "Let me introduce you, Mr. Holmes."

"Thank you," Spencer said, as he made a small nod at Mr. Dihje, who had anticipated him, and withdrew a notebook and pen from his jacket.

She pointed at each one as she spoke, moving clockwise around the collection.

"This is Harold Fleischakel. He was a very kind man, a great gentleman. He owned a large winery in Napa Valley, which he loved. His mood rose and fell with the success of each year's crop. He was built like a peasant, and always had the deep tan of a gardener, with long, silver hair and a planter's hat. He taught me an appreciation of wine. He used to bring me bottles of wine with my own label. But his particular interest was sailing. We usually spent Fridays on the bay, if the weather was favorable. He was the first I met, in January of 1961. I was just eighteen.

"This is Carl Marchand. He owned Marchand's, a big department store on Market Street. He was extremely refined, cultured. He made the retail business seem like an art gallery sometimes. He was thin and always impeccably well-dressed. He had the soul of an artist, I suppose, and was always frustrated that he had gone into business instead of following his first love, which was music. He was always trying to encourage performing companies in the city. He took me to the opera on our night together. Thursdays. We had season tickets. I had to nudge him sometimes, because he would hum along unconsciously.

"This tall man with the beard is Stephen Douglas Turner, who was a successful attorney. He had an office in the financial district. Turner, Bachman and Turner, I think it was. He loved to play chess, and taught me. We usually spent our nights—Mondays—at home. We played chess, and he liked to read to me. He had a cute little potbelly that he was always threatening to do something about. And he managed my money for me. He made arrangements for me to own this house, provided my allowance, and turned over some properties that were left to me by the others.

"This is Robert Perlmutter; he owned a fleet of taxi cabs. He was the most fun to be with, always a joke, and very generous. He was always giving me jewelry. They're pretty old-fashioned pieces, but I still have them all. Every Tuesday night we toured the nightclubs, dancing and seeing the shows. He loved the big bands, and the singers. Loved to dance. He was everybody's friend.

"This is Billy Hansen. 'Little Billy' everyone called him. He was a jockey before I knew him, had retired, and had built up a stable of racehorses. He bred them. He had a ranch on the Russian River. He taught me to ride, and we spent Wednesdays riding in Golden Gate Park. He was very small and wiry, with an intense energy. It just seemed to emanate from him all the time.

"Bobby died in 1967, then Carl and Billy in '69, Harold in '75, and Stevie in '81. They were never here together, except once a year on my birthday. Here's a photograph of the six of us at the last get-together that was complete. It seems a long time ago now."

Spencer gazed at the childlike girl in the center of the five distinguished men. It was difficult to recognize her as the self-assured woman who stood beside him now.

"After Bobby died, I saw the others for a little while, but they were getting on and seemed to be losing enthusiasm. Not for me—they were always very caring—but for life in general, I guess. They had been friends for half a century, since World War I. Here's a picture of the platoon on Armistice Day. They said they wanted it to hang here, so I would know how young and handsome they once were. They were silly about that. They never knew how much I really loved them. I guess I had a thing for older men. My own father was never a part of my life, but the few times I saw him he was a dashing figure, and I worshiped him. Put all together, these five men offered just about everything a young girl could want. At the time I thought it would last forever."

"After the girl was born, you just went on as before?"

"Oh yes. She was born in '67 and I came right back here."

"And you never saw your child again?"

"Never." Again Spencer thought he detected a fractional hesitation. She looked at him squarely.

"You must think me a terribly immoral woman, Mr. Holmes. All I can say—"

"No, no, not at all. I do not judge my fellow men—or women—so harshly as you might think. Your arrangement is—was—your own business. Clearly it was to both your benefit and the benefit of the five men. As it hurt no one else, no one has cause to complain. My investigations are only concerned with those people who have trespassed on the rights of their fellow man."

"Thank you, Mr. Holmes. But I was not referring to my arrangement as a young prostitute and mistress. I may have made some unusual choices in my life, but I feel no need to defend them. In any case, my life has worked out rather well, I think. As you say, it is no one's business but my own. I was referring to the fact that I abandoned my child. That was a terrible mistake."

They had wandered back to the living room and all stood in front of the fireplace.

"It may interest you to know," Spencer proffered, "that she was well taken care of by a loving and rather advantaged family. The result seems to me to be a well-adapted and happily situated young woman. She will survive this tragedy, I am sure."

"Unfortunately, all that does not change the fact that she was abandoned at birth. It may not have affected her, but it affected me some years later. I suddenly realized I was child-less. And yet I had given birth. Do you have children, Mr. Holmes?"

"I don't."

"Then you can't know. Not *really* know, I mean. I have taken to volunteering several days a week at the children's hospital on 19th Avenue. It is an extraordinary experience. The youngest are so bewildered, so giving, so trusting. You cannot look in their eyes without feeling some sense of responsibility. The connection is almost primordial, I'm sure. I can't explain it, and perhaps a man cannot feel it."

Neither of the two unmarried bachelors had a response to Sarah's small but passionate disclosure. The three shifted uncomfortably for a moment.

"Well," Sarah said, "I've told you about my five friends. I wish I could help, but . . ."

"You've been very helpful, Ms. Bernstein. Thank you for filling us in on the girl's history. It may come in handy."

"Surely it was the boy someone intended to shoot?"

"I think so. But as the timing was most unusual, we believe the wedding itself to be connected in some way. That is why we wanted to investigate the girl's background somewhat. Just in case. For her own protection."

"If there's anything else I can do . . . ?"

"We'll be in touch."

"All right."

Following the shaking of hands all around, and courteous pleasantries, Spencer and Mr. Dihje were shown to the door.

Chapter 10

*Not to worry, Spencer and Mr. Dihje return
in time for their supper.*

Outside on the sidewalk, Spencer stopped a moment to look
back at the cozy house.

"A curious woman," he remarked casually.

"Hiding something, I think," Dihje responded.

"Oh, yes. She knows more about her daughter than she ad-
mits. She knows who the girl is today, and was well aware, even
before we arrived, of the shooting at the girl's wedding. Did
you notice?"

"She say boy shot at wedding. We not tell her."

"Exactly. She knew about the shooting at the wedding of her
daughter. Ergo, she knows that her infant Felicity Bernstein is
the young lady Felicity Harrington. She has lived not five miles
from her own daughter all her life. And however long she has
known it, she certainly knew it by last Sunday. Yet somehow I
trust her. Such an honest woman, didn't you think? Too honest
even to lie convincingly when I asked her if she knew where her
baby was. Well, we shall see . . ."

From the car, Spencer dialed the Pinkerton office. There
were no new developments. They drove home.

"I'm afraid the trail is cold for the time being. We'll have
more to chew over soon, I'm sure. In the meantime, how about
that pheasant?"

Chapter 11

In which Spencer gathers the thin threads of the case to date, and attempts to weave a tapestry.

It was midnight when Spencer Holmes retired to his study to ponder what he considered a three-pipe problem.

Mr. Dihje, having climbed the circular staircase that led from the kitchen to his own room on the second floor, had retired for the night, and lay in bed under a small lamp, chuckling over an episode of *The Honeymooners.* The big house was quiet. The streets of the residential neighborhood were empty. A chill night air enveloped the mansion, and the mist began to roll in from the Pacific, blanketing the city and the bay at its feet.

As Spencer prepares his first pipe, we might remark on his surroundings. Unlike most of the mansion, which displays the sure hand of a talented, if theatrical, interior decorator, the room in which our man mulls appears haphazardly appointed. The one room it does not imitate, we hasten to add, is the notorious sitting room of his grandfather. No mantelpiece features unanswered correspondence transfixed with a jackknife, no coal grate holds cigars, nor is there a Persian slipper containing his tobacco mixture.

Instead, a white marble fireplace features only a graceful ebony dancer circa 1925. Hanging above it, a large color reproduction of the inside of Sutro Baths represents a long-gone but once-favorite local landmark. The wallpaper, a subtle gray fabric rather than red-flocked, is not pocked with bullet holes (although a large VR is featured on a target posted in the basement pistol range). Along one wall an early model of a pinball machine glows. A large aquarium provides a comfortable home for a single Siamese fighting fish. Crossed swords hang on the wall, but they are modern foils well used. Bausch & Lomb binoculars hang by the window for perusing the city below, and an enormous reflector telescope points to the universe above.

Various unidentified artifacts lie haphazardly on the overstuffed couch, chair, and table, but whether they each represent a clue upon which some successfully resolved case had turned, or simply the impedimenta of a restless and inquisitive mind, only their collector knows. A skull with a candle in it sits on an end table. This fell into Spencer's possession as the result of his investigations into a local black-magic coven which had extended its talents to the importation of cocaine through its Haitian connections.

The man before us, placidly contemplating two murders, sits in an antique barber's chair in front of a large window that exposes a good portion of his favorite city.

Although Spencer is the first to acknowledge his grandfather's considerable contribution to the methods upon which he and his contemporaries depend, and has even been known to repeat a quotation out of sheer idolatry for the well-turned phrase, he makes no serious attempt to impersonate his famous forebear. At the moment, for example, he relaxes in a black silk Nehru jacket and black gabardine slacks, and puffs at a hand-carved pipe. The jacket is far out of date, but had been a gift from the man who gave it his name, and Spencer would not part with it to fit the current fashions.

Any suspicion that he dwells in the past will be firmly put to rest by the presence of the Macintosh computer that sits on the glass-topped, Bauhaus desk in the center of the room. Although in awe, with the rest of the world, of his grandfather's extraordinary powers of observation, Spencer is the first to recognize the tremendous complexity of the modern world. That even a diligent and inquiring mind could hope to catalogue a fraction of the scientific information added to the world's knowledge since the reign of Queen Victoria is not possible. Spencer's iconoclastic attachment to facts had to be serviced in a more modern way. Hence the computer. With it, and the modem at its side, Spencer can roam freely through a storehouse of information collected in memory banks throughout the world. More facts, lists, references, encyclopedias, directo-

ries, quantifications, catalogues, registers, rolls, rosters, and
schedules were available to him than could ever have been contained in the entire British Museum. Much less in one man's
mind, however roomy.

Truth be told, expediency was not the sole satisfaction Spencer received from his Mac. In spite of the computer's reputation for complex technicality, its elegant monitor afforded
Spencer, in effect, a palette. His paints were facts and figures,
but as he called them up, shifted them around, alphabetized,
collated, and construed them, they became a collage of information that formed, like the thousands of tiny bytes in the
central processing unit, a picture so much larger—the Big Picture, Spencer called it—that the individual bits of information
were obscured, like the dots of an impressionist's painting.
When the flick of a few keys popped lists, photos, names, or
even theories on his screen, Spencer felt at his most creative.
Just now the screen was blank, however, and his eyes, if not his
attention, were turned to the Bay beyond his window.

The scene on which Spencer gazes without seeing is equally
eccentric. On his left, graceful red arches swathed in fog span
the gateway to the Pacific. To his right, atop Telegraph Hill, a
shocking phallic symbol rises tumescently toward the sky. Directly before him, the aging walls of Alcatraz penitentiary sit
on a somber island, quiet and deserted. The prison had been
closed down in 1963 and Spencer for one thought it a pity. The
stone fortress that once housed such notables as Al Capone and
The Birdman would, if it were still active, give his view from
this room a satisfying quality, representing as it did the proper
setting for the miscreants of society.

Presently, he allows the calm night Bay scene in front of him
to organize his thoughts.

A boy had been audaciously murdered, poised on the very
edge of matrimony, on stage in front of several hundred witnesses, in the middle of a sun-drenched afternoon.

A man had been surreptitiously murdered, in the very act of
adultery, on stage with no witnesses, in the middle of the dark
night.

The boy's young fiancée was at the dawn of her maidenhood,
sweet, innocent, from a world of wealth and privilege.

The man's paramour was on that familiar slide toward the

depths of degradation, cynical, wanton, a drifter on the edge of a scurrilous society.

Nothing to date had connected these two bizarre assassinations, yet Spencer's instincts told him that only one man could be so calculating, so clever, so conniving. He knew that before long a clue would appear that would elucidate the connection. Until then, he would seek to discover a possible motivation the killer might have had. Therein lay the key, for someone had gone to altogether too much trouble for ordinary gains. There was something substantial at stake, and halfway through his third pipeful of imported hashish, Spencer had a vague glimmer of what it might be.

Chapter 12

The obituary brings Spencer another clue.

The death of a winemaker confirmed his theory. This information came to him the next day. He was perusing the morning papers when a small item from the Wines and Spirits column caught his notice:

CHAMPION WINEMAKER DEAD

Randal Fleischakel, 58, President of Essex Vintners, Napa, drowned last night in a barrel of cabernet sauvignon '85 being prepared for fermentation. Apparently Fleischakel, a dedicated winemaker and successful architect of the corporate expansion of his father's vineyards, was examining a solution of recently crushed grapes when he lost his balance and fell into the barrel. He was discovered the next morning by his foreman in the course of drawing off the skins from the surface of the mixture.

Harold Fleischakel had built the winery in 1937 after migrating to the valley from Eastern Europe. His son Randal had been President since the death of the founder in 1975.

Randal Fleischakel first gained prominence in 1980 with the unveiling of a California chardonnay which took the blue ribbon in France's prestigious wine competition.

He is survived by his widow, the Swedish model Heidi Lundstrom, who he met on a wine-tasting tour of Europe in 1982. There are no children.

Fleischakel had last year sold his winery to Amalgamated Wines and Spirits, but continued as its President.

An Amalgamated spokesman said no unusual difficulties were expected with this year's cabernet as a result of the accident.

Spencer folded the newspaper, placed it on the table, and rang for his confidant.

Chapter 13

Wherein the tempo of events quickens considerably.

"My suspicion that the murder of the groom was engineered to prevent the marriage is confirmed. It is the girl and not the unfortunate young man upon whom the mystery settles. The son of one of her fathers has been murdered. It is not possible to drown in cabernet sauvignon. It is far too buoyant a wine. Also there would be no reason for Fleischakel to taste a wine that had not yet been fermented. It would simply be grape juice. Our man becomes cleverer and cleverer. The background of our lascivious quintet becomes increasingly the focus of our attention."

Using a private telephone number and his modem, Spencer connected to an information bank downtown, and within a few minutes had read off the green monitor the names of living relatives of the five deceased satyrs. Each of the men had a son born during the 1920's and 1930's. Randal Fleischakel, deceased winemaker, had been one of those sons, but it was Harris Perlmutter who set Spencer's adrenaline flowing.

"Good heavens, here it is, right in front of my nose, and I've overlooked it until now."

Mr. Dihje, with his exceptional instinct for the ebb and flow of an investigation, ran to Spencer's side. He leaned over to read the screen.

"Don't you see it! Harry Pearl was Harris Perlmutter, son of Robert Perlmutter. He changed his name. And a good thing, too, dragging the name of his father into the Barbary Coast. No one is born a Pearl; it should have rung a bell yesterday when I first heard the names. Pearl, the first to be killed, was a descendant of one of Miss Bernstein's suitors, as was Randal. The second killing followed almost immediately. And both men were eldest sons."

Spencer searched quickly through the information on the monitor.

"See here, there are three more. They are in great danger. We must fly!"

With the aide of the local telephone directory, the detective ascertained that the three remaining men all resided within the boundaries of the city proper. He jotted down their addresses, stuffed the paper in his pocket, and headed for the elevator.

It was not in Spencer's nature to drive a Rolls-Royce recklessly. When the two men reached the garage they climbed into a Volkswagen bug, which had the virtues of anonymity, parking ease, and a Porsche engine, the insertion of which allowed it to assume speeds in excess of ninety miles per hour. Spencer wheeled this vehicle into the street and shot quickly for the Russian Hill address of the eldest son of William Hansen.

Chapter 14

In which Spencer meets one of the Weekday Club descendants.

The sixty-five-year-old man was in excellent health. This was demonstrated by the fact that he had completed eighty sit-ups and was heading for the century mark when the butler ushered Spencer Holmes and Sowhat Dihje into his private gymnasium. He called out "one hundred" and settled back. Spencer extended his business card. The sexagenarian athlete took it firmly, read it, and handed it back. He moved to a rug and stood over a silver bar bulging ominously with weights. He hefted the bar to chin level, then began pressing it overhead, the strain popping out the veins in his neck. Perspiration rolled down his forehead. At the same time, he spoke.

"A detective, huh? I suppose you represent Lily. I've got a message for her; you can take it."

"Mr. Hansen, you're mis—"

"Just listen. Lily walked out on me and when she did she took the car and left me the key to the house. All right. She can keep the car. But that's it. She gets not one more penny. And if she tries anything in court, she gets a surprise and so do you. I got in my collection a few photographs of that broad the judge will be interested in. She's not the only one in the picture. So you can forget about that old business. As far as community property goes, she got the car and it was paid for. This house isn't and there isn't much else. I know she thinks I'm holding out on her but that's her problem. That about gives you the whole picture." He dropped the weights suddenly, and Spencer and Mr. Dihje jumped back. "Now if you don't mind, I've got a few miles to do."

With this dismissal, the man walked swiftly across the gymnasium and disappeared through a door on the other side. Spencer and Mr. Dihje hurried after him and found themselves standing on the sidewalk outside the town house. Looking both ways, they spotted the man just turning the corner at the bottom of the street. They sprinted after him.

In a moment they were able to pull alongside. Hansen was doing seven-minute miles. This presented no difficulty for Spencer, who was in excellent condition, even if his style imitated a crane taking off, but the shorter legs of Mr. Dihje were pumping twice as fast. The trio began to circle the park, with Spencer forced to shout over the beating of their hearts.

"I do not deal in cases of divorce or disaffection. This is a matter of murder. We have reason to believe you are in grave danger."

"Don't threaten me, mister. I told you—"

"No, no, you misunderstand. We do not represent Miss Lily, whoever she may be. We are investigating the murder of two men who may have been innocent of anything other than being descendants of a group of friends. Your father was a member of that group. You may be the next intended victim of someone who is attempting to carry out a vindictive plot of some sort."

The man stopped. Dihje, for one, was greatly relieved.

"What sort?"

"I beg your pardon?"

"What sort of plot, man! What are you talking about?"

"Oh. Well, that's a bit of a problem still. I haven't uncovered it entirely."

"Who got themselves killed?"

"Randal Fleischakel, son of your father's friend Harold Fleischakel, the winery owner. And Harry Pearl, son of Robert Perlmutter, also a friend of your father."

"I'll tell you something, Stretch. If you're trying to buffalo me, you've got the wrong mark." And with that Robert Hansen touched his toes three times in quick succession and took off running again. While Spencer kept up, Mr. Dihje struggled gamely to stay within earshot.

"Five men were in business together," Spencer shouted, now fighting the noise of traffic as they exited the park and jogged along the sidewalk. "Your father was one of them. Each had a son. Two of those sons have died in freak accidents."

"Sounds pretty speculative to me."

"I admit there are a number of holes in the theory at this point."

"What business was my father in with this group?"

"A rather delicate one, actually. A sort of cooperative. A sort of health club for the soul, you might say."

"You don't make a lot of sense, Stretch."

"You must listen to me. You are one of the three remaining eldest sons of these five men. I have strong suspicions—"

Robert Hansen stopped suddenly.

"Suspicions! What do you want me to do, go on a long ocean voyage? Jump at my own shadow? Look at me, sixty-five years old and I can take any punk off the street. I can bench-press 250 pounds and run a mile in under five minutes. I'm in the pink. Nothing's going to happen to me, I can tell you."

Those far-from-prophetic words were the last Spencer, or anyone else for that matter, was to hear from Robert Hansen. For at their conclusion, the man clutched his heart, rolled his eyes upwards, and collapsed on the street.

Cardiopulmonary resuscitation, in which both Spencer and Mr. Dihje were well trained, had no effect. Mr. Hansen was pronounced dead on arrival at the hospital. More likely, he was dead when he landed supine on the pavement beneath his Nike-soled feet.

Chapter 15

A sinister smell confirms Spencer's suspicions.

A crowd had gathered and watched the small drama. This is a standard, ghoulish, if understandable, aspect of voyeurism, wherein the onlookers are able, however subconsciously, to say to themselves, "Better him than me." Now they were reluctant to depart the scene, even though the corpse had been carted away.

"Curiouser and curiouser," pronounced Spencer, in unconscious imitation of a much-admired Oxford don and friend of his grandfather's. Half an hour later, the paramedics having delivered the body to city facilities, he and Mr. Dihje stood on the pavement gazing down on the blank space where the body of Robert Hansen had landed. Although there was no etched outline, the figure was nevertheless luminescent for Spencer, who felt some sense of failure over his having been unable to convince Mr. Hansen of his imminent mortality. They stood gazing at the vanished effigy for no little time.

At last Spencer bent down. He sniffed.

He placed a finger on the pavement in a barely discernible cavity formed by the uneven cement. Closer examination had given light to a dampness that ought to have evaporated by noon.

"Fairy glove. The sweet smell of dried leaves of the Digitalis Purpurea."

Spencer now presented the eccentric figure of a man on his hands and knees on the steep sidewalk of a busy San Francisco street. A few bystanders still lingered leisurely, and to their satisfaction, the detective was now examining a portion of the sidewalk with a large magnifying glass which had appeared from beneath his coat. His assistant, still upright, presented an equally exotic silhouette as he scanned the horizon through a pair of collapsible binoculars. When their examinations were complete, the two men sauntered off down the hill and the crowd reluctantly dispersed.

"Did you happen to notice," Spencer muttered, "the Morris Minor that was parked at the corner on the other side of the street when we first crossed out of the park? It seems to be gone now. I believe it drove off just after the ambulance arrived."

The ungarrulous Mr. Dihje remarked neither on his own observation of the automobile nor his assumption that it might have some bearing on the case. It might be assumed that he had observed its suspicious behavior, however, for from his prodigious memory he produced a single piece of information, which was offered to Spencer in the understated manner of a butler proffering a dish of vegetables to Lord Emsworth: he quietly recited the license plate number of the vehicle in question.

Chapter 16

A night at the opera.

That evening Spencer Holmes and Mr. Dihje chose to attend the opera. They arrived fashionably attired in white tie and tails, with Spencer sporting an accompanying cape.

Their objective, however, was not to luxuriate amid the glorious sounds echoing about the rococo splendor of the War Memorial Opera House. They had already been in attendance on opening night of the production (which Spencer had found a trifle too traditional for his taste). Instead they circled behind the building, crossed the parking lot to the artists' entrance and entered the backstage area, where they circulated freely amid the hubbub of what might, in this case, be appropriately titled Behind the Scenes in Egypt.

The two men blended easily into the hustle and bustle, for they were familiar faces backstages. This was due to the occasional duty they performed onstage as supers, for the sheer pleasure of standing among, as opposed to sitting before, such splendid examples of the human voice at its most gloriously musical. Tonight, the hectic corridors verged as always on the completely chaotic.

They were endeavoring to come face-to-face with the owner of the automobile that Mr. Dihje had recently catalogued. A call to a contact in the bureaucratic bowels of the California Department of Motor Vehicles in Sacramento had elicited a name and address. Inquiries made of a gregarious landlady had established the fact that its owner was employed at the opera house, backstage division. That the name of the man in question was Freddy Marchand, firstborn son of Carl Marchand of the Bernstein circle, had given them a fierce sense of purpose.

Marchand, it turned out, was a stagehand with the opera, and Spencer and Dihje bearded him at his habitual occupation: playing five-card stud with his comrades in the basement directly underneath the pyramids of the Nile. He was startled to see them certainly, but showed little inclination to take it on the lam. Spencer, in fact, had some difficulty persuading him to step aside and enter into a discussion, engaged as he was in the delicate task of attempting to fill an inside straight. This satisfactorily completed, he accompanied Spencer and Mr. Dihje to a corner where a giant gong stood unused. While Mr. Dihje, a devotee of that exotic instrument, fingered it lovingly, Spencer went on the attack.

"See here, my good man. We know perfectly well that you were parked at the corner of Hyde and Greenwich this afternoon. You took off—suspiciously, I might add—immediately on the heels of a commotion resulting from the demise of Robert Hansen. What were you doing loitering in those circumstances?"

The man answered with a casual alacrity that belied Spencer's belief in his culpability.

"I thought you two were the ones. So you saw me, too, eh? Well, sure, I was there all right. So what?"

"Mr. Hansen was murdered. I'm sure the authorities will find that he suffered a fatal heart attack. But we believe it was induced. You were on the scene. And you are connected with not only Mr. Hansen, but with two other men whose death certificates do not contain an adequate description of the circumstances which led them to their final resting place. In short, I have every reason to believe you are guilty of murder."

"You're outta your mind. I was sitting in the car waiting for Hansen to get back. I knocked on the door and that butler said he was out jogging. I thought I'd wait on the street for him to come back. I was just getting out of the car when he collapsed. And, hey, you two were right beside him all along. How do I know you didn't kill him?"

"We are characters who—as the shortcuts sometimes taken in second-rate English mystery novels might describe us—are above suspicion. You, on the other hand, must explain your actions. Either to me, now, or to the police, shortly."

"There's nothing to explain. As far as Fleischakel and Pearl go, I was here when they died. Last Sunday we had a matinee of *Salome* and I spent almost all night striking the set and putting up *Rosenkavalier*. On Monday I was running *Albert Herring* at a dress rehearsal."

"You have adequate witnesses to your participation?"

"Sure. The whole crew."

"Hmm . . . yes, I see what you mean. Given the propensity among sceneshifters to require double the necessary number of hands adequate to the task, and their customary habit of standing around a good deal observing one another, I suppose you have a cast-iron alibi. Nevertheless, you seem to know a good deal about the timing of the two deaths. And you were present at the scene when Hansen drew his last aerobic breath. Explain yourself."

"Well, it's simple. I went to see him about that goddamn will."

It was with these words that the tone of the conversation, indeed of the entire investigation, took a sudden turn. A will, that instrument documenting the various stubborn, eccentric, and whimsical traits of the elderly, was so illuminating a piece of evidence in so many dark and sinister cases that Spencer had to fight to keep from betraying his enthusiasm for this change of fortune. He willed his eyebrows to stay in place. Mr. Dihje turned from his inspection of the center resonating space of the gong, and, making no change in his expression, fastened his attention upon the suspect.

"The will?" was all Spencer allowed himself to say at this delicate juncture.

"You must know about the will. You're investigating the deaths of Fleischakel, Pearl, and Hansen, aren't you?"

"We are. Their connection with each other, and you, stems from the coincidence that each of you are the firstborn male son of a group of elderly men engaged in a curious partnership some time ago. All are now deceased. I am currently attempting to reconstruct that arrangement, for reasons that I am not at liberty to make clear to you. Explain to me, if you will, the details of this will."

"Does your friend always talk like this?" the stagehand said to Mr. Dihje, who remained implacable. Mr. Dihje's knowledge of the English language being sketchy still, and the majority of his experience being with his American sponsor, it is unlikely that he recognized anything unusual in his employer's semantics. The stagehand, in any case, continued.

"The old men you're talking about, who included my crazy father, left a trust fund for their eldest sons. They each contributed $20,000. That's $100,000. It's what they call a 'tontine.' It hasn't been touched in over twenty years. It amounts to over a million dollars now. I just checked with the bank."

"And a tontine," Spencer said by way of continuing the narration in its most likely direction, "goes to the last surviving legatee. Things are becoming clearer now. With the deaths of Fleischakel, Pearl, and Hansen, only two firstborn sons remain: you and Turner. Whoever predeceases the other leaves the remaining man to collect a cool million. More than enough cold cash to induce murderous circumstances."

It was at this particular point that, had we been present, we might have noticed a certain shift in the equanimity of Freddy Marchand. His face clouded over. His eyes deepened and shifted erratically. His brow perspired. He began to look for a more comfortable positioning for his center of gravity.

"You really think those guys were killed?"

"I know it."

"The paper said Pearl had an accident. And Fleischakel drowned. Hansen had a heart attack. You saw it yourself."

"They were murdered. The rest was window dressing."

"You think someone is trying to collect the million?"

"Weren't you?"

"Well, not like that. I read about Fleischakel and Pearl dying. I knew there were only the three of us left. I went over to see Hansen. I had an idea that we could break the trust if we agreed, collect a third of a million each. I'm the youngest, you know, so I was offering something when you think about it."

"What about Turner?"

"I thought Hansen and I'd get together and go to him with the proposal. He's a lawyer, I don't trust him too much. Say . . ."

"Yes, I see you've tumbled to the situation. You and Turner are the only two left. There is a significant probability that one of you, having gone this far, need only kill the other."

It was these remarks that triggered a sudden and considerable increase in Marchand's already rising agitation. Whether he felt in physical danger, knowing he had not to date engaged in murder, and thus was the next target, or whether he had masterminded the situation, and now felt the jig in all probability was up, could not be discerned. Spencer treaded lightly. Dihje moved quietly into a position which might be more advantageous should the man attempt to escape.

"You understand that a man guilty of murder cannot collect an inheritance which comes to him as a result of his illegal activities?"

"Does Turner know that?"

"Meaning, I take it, to throw suspicion on him and away from yourself."

"I told you I was here when Fleischakel and Pearl died. And how do you think I gave Hansen a heart attack—scared him from the corner? You two were right there. How did that happen, huh?"

"At this point I have only a theory. The autopsy should tell us more. In the meantime, if your alibi for the deaths of Pearl and Fleischakel proves correct, then Mr. Turner, whom I have not yet had the pleasure to meet, does seem to be in the hot seat at this time."

"Yeah. And where is he now? That's what I want to know."

At this point a bell rang in the basement and Spencer recognized the signal for an impending scene change. The stagehands, exhibiting a level of activity which until now might have seemed outside their capacities, leapt up from their positions around the felt-covered barrel and shot up the stairs. Freddy glanced over his shoulder.

"Shit. I gotta go."

Spencer calculated quickly.

"Mr. Dihje shall accompany you. He is familiar with the backstage machinery of this house as well as the libretto in question, and thus will not be in the way. If any questions are asked, you may say he is a bona fide member of the union. We will not mention it is the Bombay local. It is for your own protection."

"Suit yourself."

Freddy Marchand, with Mr. Dihje on his heels, headed up the stairway after his confederates. Spencer did not make public the concluding portion of his thoughts: that it was also for the protection of Stephen Douglas Turner. For Spencer, in spite of the protestations of Marchand, was not altogether convinced of Turner's culpability. There was much more to these circumstances, he was sure, than had yet to meet the eye.

Freed for the moment from the efforts his investigations had so far entailed, he perambulated to the nearest pay phone.

There he waited as a young lady, whose excellent figure was being shown to good advantage thanks to a costume designer's interpretation of the pajamas worn by the girls in the harem of the King of Egypt, discussed in an agitated manner the failure of a certain saxophone player, from some less esoteric musical establishment, to show up as promised following last night's performance. Apparently unwilling to give him a second chance tonight, she slammed down the receiver.

The young woman quite obviously was going to be free for the evening. Spencer was silently considering the idea of volunteering to fill the engagement which had been denied the woodwinder, when she turned around suddenly, nearly colliding with him. He was thus yanked out of a reverie that had reached the stage of a bird and a bottle at Maurice et Charles. Their tête-à-tête was launched with an aggressive exclamation by the young lady:

"Musicians! The worst!"

"I play the piano," volunteered Spencer, "but have lately undertaken to learn the violin. It is a family obligation, you might say," Spencer sighed, trying to maintain his pose of equanimity.

"Yeah? Oh, well, that's a very refined instrument."

"Indeed."

"I mean, you can't improvise on a violin. You can't stay up until three in the morning riffing a blues chorus, and leave your date standing out in the cold."

"Actually, there is a man named Stéphane Grappelli who did some remarkable things with his violin while engaged by the Hot Club in Paris, and undoubtedly much of his playing took place during the wee hours. Of course, deviating from the line laid down by, say, Mozart, would surely have no positive use. Then there is country-western music, but here we might probably be allowed to distinguish between the 'fiddle' and the 'violin.' Oh, but excuse me, I see I have once again overindulged my habit of speculation."

The woman was speechless, her blue eyes glued to Spencer. Her dark hair fell to her shoulders. Her ivory face had more than a touch of the exotic. Spencer's experience with theatrical makeup enabled him to envision the more innocent features that lay underneath the rich application of indigo-blue eye shadow. He was impressed with what he imagined.

The girl sighed. This caused the upper expanse of her bosom to float toward Spencer, then recede. She lowered triple eyelashes to take in the full figure of the man, then returned to his face, and finally found her tongue.

"Are you with the orchestra? I don't know many people in the string section."

"Alas, no. I have only just undertaken that difficult instrument, and play the piano for my private pleasure only."

"Oh."

Spencer, unaccustomed to volunteering information, let a moment go by before continuing. It was adequately filled by what, in romantic fiction, would be described as gazing into one another's eyes.

"Actually, I'm just visiting backstage. I have supered here, though. And I visited often as a child. My mother performed here some years ago."

"Maybe I knew her?"

"She was before your time, I'm sure. How long have you been singing here?"

"Two years. I just graduated from the San Francisco Conservatory. I'm a soprano in the chorus."

"I'm sure you'll be promoted in no time."

"Thank you, but you haven't heard me sing."

"I can tell by your speaking voice. It is rich and unique. The Conservatory is a splendid training program. And the Maestro here does not tolerate anything less than perfection. It is one of the high points of our city's cultural life. Ergo, you have an exceptional future."

"You make it sound so reasonable."

"I know the profession you have chosen is an extremely competitive one. You must keep up your courage."

"Are you a buff?"

"Opera is certainly one of my interests. Are you familiar with the role of Lakmed? You would be eminently suited for it."

"I sang it my senior year! Do you know *Giovanni*?"

"Donna Anna. A splendid role."

" 'Non me dir' was my audition piece."

"An excellent choice. You had no trouble with the ending?"

"No, I can go to a D without closing. Of course, I'm no Ponselle, but I'm working."

"You're too modest."

Here we might discontinue our eavesdropping. As will be guessed by the preceding, the conversation was of the sort which tends to entertain the participants, but falls flat on the ears of an outsider, due to certain enharmonic feelings between them that are incomprehensible to others. Indeed, whether the two were exchanging information on soprano roles or discussing the weather would have made no difference at all. Their conversation, infused as it was with a rarefied air and Freudian tension, would have been equally stimulating to the two participants in either case.

We will content ourselves with picking up the threads of the conversation some fifteen minutes and a quarter of a mile later. The fifteen minutes can be attributed to the intermission customarily afforded the audience in the interest of avoiding the loss of their concentration due to the straining of their bladders. The distance was twice what would have been required of the lady to go from the telephone to her place in the wings, where she would be expected to enter, singing, with her fellow carolers. The extra mileage was due to the route she contrived to take in order to prolong the conversation.

We meet them again in an intimate moment, the lady with her back to a wall of ropes known in the theatre as the counterweight system, and Spencer facing her. The work under discussion is *The Impresario*.

"I had a real problem with the high F's," she admitted. "Mozart had some nerve writing five of them in a single aria. Even Sills considered it a good night if she hit four."

"I understand. But have you heard the Scotto recording? She does it so rapidly they're practically sixteenth notes, and all in one breath."

"I think that ruins the melody. The singer at the expense of the composer."

"You're right. I wouldn't ordinarily expect such reverence for the creator in one as young as yourself. Most young singers go for the fireworks."

Spencer's remarking upon her age had the effect of injecting another element into the heretofore purely academic discussion, and the girl blushed. Being a man of sensitivity, he steered the conversation back to the more sterile confines of the original ideas.

"You have a splendid career ahead of you, I'm sure. The female voice doesn't fully mature until the early thirties."

"But I've got to start singing principal roles before that or no one will take me seriously. I love the chorus, but you've got to admit there's a certain reluctance to trust the chorus singer with more responsibility."

"Conductors can be extraordinarily conservative, it's true. There is a lot of new music being written. You might demonstrate your talents through some small concerts featuring the work of younger composers. They have great difficulty getting their material heard, and for the same reason."

"A friend of mine is working on a modern opera. He wants me to sing the lead."

"How wonderful. Cosima, of course, was Wagner's mistress."

This interjection of the slightly risqué distinctly affected the conversation. The young lady blushed once again. The air between them became charged with sexual tension.

"Oh, he's just a friend. In fact, he's gay."

"I didn't mean to pry. We were talking earlier of Wagner's use of Cosima's voice."

"Myself, I'm unattached," she added.

Here the girl had managed to make a question out of a statement.

"Really?" Spencer noted.

Another pause.

"Yes."

The pauses came thick and fast now.

"And the saxophone player?"

"Who?"

It is possible that the conversation, having reached a condition bloated with pregnant pauses, might have now faltered completely, or at least disintegrated into a blushing embarrassment from which both participants would have had difficulty extricating themselves. But the situation was saved by an announcement from the stage manager (in a pretentious imitation of the British manager under which he had apprenticed) of "Beginners, please." A flurry of activity ensued, forcing Spencer and the young lady apart. By the time they found each other again, a call of "Stand by, curtain going up" had given an urgency to their conversation.

"I'll be going on soon."

"Of course. The entrance of the Priests and Priestesses."

"We must talk about Verdi next. I'm mad for him."

"Excellent! I have some rare Galli-Curci recordings. We could listen to them together."

"You never said why you were backstage tonight."

"No? I had some business with one of the grips. A Mr. Frederick Marchand. I'll be looking him up now, in fact."

"Freddy? I know he's here tonight. He must be hanging around somewhere."

As the last massive drop lowered itself into position, the stage manager called "action" and the front curtain rose. All this activity caused the ropes directly behind the girl to ride down in reaction. Attached to one of them, and replacing one hundred pounds of iron bars needed to balance the weight of the colorful rooftops of Egypt, was the inert body of Freddy Marchand. His tongue lolled out of his mouth, his eyes bulged, and his face, formerly a rosy complexion, had taken on a bluish tinge, a phenomenon undoubtedly caused by that portion of the rope wound tightly around his neck.

Chapter 17

In which Frederick Marchand appears to be eliminated from the list of suspects, leaving one.

Gli dei l'adducano
Salva alle patrie mura
E ignori la sventura
Di chi per lei morra!

There is no telling how some of the sopranos gathered in the wings would have reacted to the grotesquely swollen tongue and bulging eyeballs of Freddy Marchand, but considering the contortions they routinely put their own features to in pursuit of the perfect tone, it is possible they would have been less than shocked. In any case, a music cue caused them to surge onstage before any of them noticed the lifeless body of the stagehand hanging behind them. They were replaced, however, by others with later entrances who could not help but be transfixed by the theatrical, if gruesome, tableau.

Spencer moved quickly. In a second he was halfway up an iron ladder hidden behind the ropes. He had stayed his climb only long enough to warn the stage manager not to let anyone touch the body, though in all likelihood the stage manager on his own would have had the insight to keep everyone away from the lifeless figure, for he saw at a glance that the man's weight had been substituted for the counterweights. Unless the procedure were reversed exactly, the rooftops of Egypt would come crashing down on the heads of his cast. Just now that cast included a particularly volatile prima donna under whose abusive wrath he had more than once squirmed, and he was in no mood for a repeat performance. He contended himself with allocating various jobs to his assistants. One he sent for the police, a second he sent for the press agent, and a third he sent in search of additional counterweights. Before returning to his prompt desk, he made one other arrangement. Surreptitiously, he sent three of his sturdiest stagehands to lock the three exits from the stage house. The stage manager, a loyal reader of mysteries and an armchair detective, having secured the scene of the crime, then felt the warm glow of satisfaction, a feeling that, until now, he had only experienced vicariously. But he was also filled with apprehension. If the situation was as he surmised, the perpetrator of this particularly gruesome and public execution was caught in the fly gallery above their heads. Such an animal, when cornered, would surely be capable of anything. He kept this concern to himself, however, and did not contradict the stagehands when they began voluble speculations on the extreme clumsiness of their recently deceased cohort. Apparently those milling about the wings were convinced that their colleague's death was an industrial accident. Only the stage manager and the man in the opera cape who was disappearing into the darkness overhead were aware that there was a murderer abroad.

Next the stage manager called three lighting cues in quick succession, creating a flashing of lights which startled the principals in mid-duet and caused the soprano to crack on an E flat. With that, the lighting plot was caught up to the action and the opera was running smoothly once again. In twenty minutes he would call for the next scene change and the body of Freddy Marchand would disappear into the flies overhead. Then, thought the stage manager with some perverse territorial instinct, things would be back to normal.

Meanwhile Spencer, whose pace had slowed a bit due to the enveloping darkness, reflected on what a ludicrous figure he must have made at this moment, climbing into the flies in white tie, tails, and crepe opera cape, much like that character in the Gaston Leroux novel.

Spencer knew that a dangerous criminal was up here somewhere. There was no other way down and Spencer himself had stood facing the ladder for the ten minutes prior to the discovery of the corpse. Engrossed though he was in dialogue with the young soprano (whose name, he now realized, he had failed to ascertain), he would certainly have noticed someone climbing down. That this man was dangerous was of no concern to the impetuous Spencer, but some risk might exist for bystanders below, and he would have to be careful.

He was also worried about the safety of his faithful companion Mr. Dihje. He knew perfectly well what a meticulous man Mr. Dihje was. There was no doubt in his mind that in order to get to Marchand, someone would have had to bushwhack Sowhat Dihje with considerable conviction.

Spencer arrived on the fly floor, the grid which provided access to the rope pulley system. He stepped quietly off the ladder onto the catwalk, aware that his prey had to be somewhere in the darkness ahead. He was above even the electrical pipes, from which hung thousands of watts of illumination, and was surrounded by an impenetrable gloom, while below him onstage, due to the efforts of Giuseppe Verdi one hundred years earlier, activity was vigorous. His eyes adjusted to the darkness.

A solid wall of brick rose up behind him. The same to his right. On his left, the cavernous stage housing, containing numerous closely hung drops, was unnavigable. This left only forward, where the catwalk stretched into an inky blackness. His quarry had to be somewhere in the narrow darkness ahead.

In the rarefied heights Spencer did not hesitate. He crept forward, hoping the element of surprise might give him an advantage. Almost immediately he came upon the inert body of Mr. Dihje. He interrupted his pursuit of the fugitive to attend to the stricken Oriental.

He saw the vague outlines of his friend's arm, and fumbled in the dark until he had him by the wrist. At once he was relieved. Beneath the olive skin and strong ligaments of the man's small wrist Spencer felt a sure pulse. He turned his attention to his friend's cranium. Feeling the skull gingerly, he came to a large, tender bump behind the right ear. Thankfully, the skull was not concussed. Spencer slipped off Mr. Dihje's moccasins, and, recalling his acupuncture lessons, massaged certain points of his feet. Mr. Dihje groaned audibly and showed immediate signs of consciousness. His eyelids fluttered upwards. His eyes rolled into place. He tilted his head slightly. He focused on Spencer at last.

"A thousand apologies. My vigilance most regretful."

"Shh. Don't try to talk, my friend. The fault lies not with

you. I should have taken more precautions. This man has been one step ahead of us at every turn. Lie still and rest. I have him now."

Spencer slipped off his cape and placed it under the fine black hair, and Mr. Dihje laid back gingerly and allowed a thin sigh of breath to escape. Spencer peered into the darkness ahead of him. Music drifted up from below. Spencer remained frozen in place.

His patience was rewarded. There came a slight creak on the metal grating as someone in the distance made a move. Trusting to his instincts, and filled with the anger of a just man foiled, he jumped up and raced fearlessly ahead into the tunnel of darkness.

At once a dim, retreating figure, all in black and with a black stocking pulled over his head, appeared. Spencer increased his speed recklessly on the narrow catwalk. He launched a flying tackle that brought them both to the ground, and Spencer had him momentarily pinned to the metal grating. Before Spencer could bring the figure under control, however, the nimble fugitive rolled over, causing Spencer to slip halfway over the side of the precipice. He was forced to grab for an upright strut with one hand, and in that split second the quarry slipped away. Spencer heard his quick tread on the metal.

He leaped to his feet and followed instantly. In the blackness, enveloped by the symphonic crescendo of the music rising from below, they pounded along the catwalk, their muffled footsteps echoing.

> *La fatal pietra sovra me si chiuse*
> *Ecco la tomba mia*
> *Del di la piu non vedro*

Spencer knew he had the man trapped. The catwalk had no purpose but to provide access to the ropes along the right of the stage. It ran flush into a cement wall. He slowed down as he approached the figure in black, who stood with his back to the wall, waiting warily. Below, the music swelled to the grand finale.

Qual gemito! . . . Una larva . . .
Una vision . . . No! Forma unmana e questa
Ciel!

Spencer knew the opera was within minutes of its conclusion.
When the curtain descended the work lights would come on
and there would be enough spill on the catwalk to illuminate
the murderer.

The figure peered over the side to the stage far below. Spencer advanced warily.

Ah! Si schiude il ciel
O terra, addio, addio, valle di pianti . . .
Sogno di gaudio che in dolor svani

A noisi schiude il ciel
Si schiude il ciel e l'alme erranti
Volano al raggio dell'eterno di

The music finished. A crescendo of bravos and bravissimos
arose from the house. The desperate killer made his move. He
leaped up onto the railing, crouched on the precarious pipe,
and launched himself into space in a suicidal swan dive. Startled by the brazen maneuver, Spencer hesitated a moment before lunging forward, and the man's heels flew out of his reach.
Spencer watched the suicidal dive, then in a flash realized the
culprit's real intentions. He landed like an aerial acrobat, his
hands attached to the bottom of the heavy gold curtain, which
hung one hundred feet above the stage floor. From the balcony
a confusion of voices and pointing fingers signaled the sudden
appearance of a new character, so late in the plot, at the top of
the proscenium archway. Then the curtain began its descent.
Thunderous applause gradually gave way to puzzled silence.
The massive drapery swept downwards, lowering the hanging
figure to the stage floor. Upon arrival, the figure bounded impatiently forward. He ran to the end of the apron, leaped over the
orchestra pit, landed in a forward somersault, and raced up the
aisle to the rear of the auditorium.

Since the main curtain obstructed his view, Spencer was in
no position to observe this himself, but it was the only direction

in which the fugitive could plausibly have headed. He would shortly escape Spencer's grasp. The audience was in an uproar. The traditional "stop that man" would prove hopeless. Instead, Spencer waited impatiently at the catwalk railing until the curtain—following a rapid exchange of angry dialogue between the prima and the stage manager, who after this startling deus ex machina was unsure of what to do—rose again. Grateful for the prima's insistence upon her rightful homage, Spencer seized the opportunity presented by the bottom of the curtain, which had risen once again and was now within his line of sight. With calm nerve, he duplicated the feat of his opponent, leaped across the chasm, and attached himself to the brocade.

There he hung suspended. His descent was delayed by the extended curtain call of the prima donna, who was in no hurry to return to the line of her fellow singers, and who, each time a bouquet of roses was tossed at her feet, slowly lowered her considerable bulk to gather them to her bosom. This delay caused Spencer to hang suspended one hundred feet above the stage for some minutes, from where he spotted the figure in black disappearing through the double doors at the top of the aisle. Spencer cursed under his breath. There would be no catching up with his target now. Still, Spencer had an excellent idea of who it might be.

When the soprano at last retreated and the stage manager gave the signal to lower the curtain, Spencer came to rest on the floor. The audience, now accustomed to this unusual blocking, took less notice of him than they had of his predecessor.

Spencer raced up the aisle and burst through the double doors. By the time he reached the veranda outdoors, however, there was no sign of the man anywhere. He had disappeared into the darkness of the city night.

Chapter 18

In which a wrap-up of the evening's events returns everyone to their own preoccupations.

Backstage, much had taken place since the lifeless body of Mr. Frederick Marchand had first been discovered. The prima donna had expressed her outrage over being upstaged during her bow, and having to miss out on the wild adulation available. The singers, stagehands, and musicians, eager to return to their homes for the evening, had flooded back to their dressing rooms, then quickly left the building. The assistant stage manager, who had been sent to contact the police, had been delayed when he came across a lovely young ballerina with no entrances scheduled in the final act, and their activity had put the counterweights out of his mind. The press agent had, after some searching, been found at a nearby watering hole bracing himself for tomorrow's arrival of an infamously temperamental tenor. His condition was insufficiently sober for any understanding of the circumstances. The stage manager had gone about his usual business of closing down for the night, with a checklist long enough to put the recent incident out of his mind.

Consequently, when the small remaining crew struck the set for the evening, and the rooftops of Egypt were sent back into the flies, the now-cold body of the well-hung Mr. Marchand descended silently into the wings, this time arriving at a deserted backstage area.

The crew and stage manager disappeared through an upstage archway and made their way home. The electrician, unaware of any untoward happenings, except the late calling of three light cues, hung up his headset, shut down all but a single lamp from his control panel on the opposite side, and passed out the stage door. Only the ancient doorman, known to one and all as Pops, remained. He might come across Freddy on his rounds. But arthritis and rheumatism having curtailed much of his assigned route in the last few years, this was not necessarily likely.

Mr. Dihje, nursing a pounding headache, climbed down the iron ladder. He walked over to the stiffening body of Freddy Marchand and stood facing it for a moment. As it hung lifeless, drifting in a lethargic spin, Mr. Dihje thought about the daily violence to which his adopted country seemed so addicted. Yet Mr. Dihje believed that death was not final at all, but merely a station stop in the continuing evolution of one's soul. Perhaps, he thought, the soul of Freddy Marchand, whatever guilt or innocence it harbored, would soon make a reappearance.

Finally he meandered out the exit. Under the first street lamp he noticed a pretty young woman hesitating between the stage door and the streetcar stop, apparently holding out hope for the arrival of a stage-door Johnny. Whoever she was, Mr. Dihje sympathized with her. Lacking exact change for a municipal bus, he wandered home on foot. His failure to protect a living clue to the mystery his employer was attempting to unravel weighed heavily on him. Never since his arrival in this bewildering civilization had he felt so lonely and depressed.

Chapter 19

Spencer closes the net.

Following the performance, Spencer alone had engaged in activity that might be useful for us to follow. He raced to the nearest pay phone and put in a call to the Pinkerton office. Within twenty minutes a pair of operatives had staked out a house on Telegraph Hill. No one would enter or leave without their knowledge.

By midnight Spencer Holmes had arrived at the scene. Recognizing him, both operatives stepped out from behind their assigned bushes. The men spoke in lowered voices.

"Mr. Holmes? It's me, Louis."

"Good evening, gentlemen. When did you arrive?"

"11:17. No one has come out. One man entered at 11:35. He wore evening clothes. The lights went on in that window there. He's been sitting at that desk ever since."

"How did he come?"

"By taxi. Didn't seem to be in a big hurry."

"Nothing else?"

"He wasn't carrying anything, except a playbill."

"Could you see it?"

"Aida."

Spencer looked up the steep hill at a series of small houses tucked underneath the trees. He picked out the house he wanted, a blue cottage laced with ivy, and stared at the window for a long time.

"I'm going in. No one leaves. Especially him."

The men returned to the bushes. Spencer climbed the steps and approached the cottage door. Above a small glowing bell, a white card in a brass frame announced the name of the homeowner: Stephen Douglas Turner, Jr. Here was the fifth of the

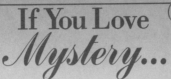

Use Your Powers of Deduction!

Follow these clues to the "World of Mystery," and enjoy Agatha Christie like you've never enjoyed her before!

Clue #1—The World's Greatest Mysteries!

Intrigue...murder...deception! No one does it like Dame Agatha! Now savour her most cunning tales of mystery and mayhem in *The Agatha Christie Mystery Collection*.

Clue #2—Beautiful Volumes!

These are collector's editions—not available in any bookstore. Bound in sturdy, simulated leather of rich, Sussex blue, set off with distinctive gold embossing in the finest Victorian tradition. Covers are densely padded—elegant on the shelf, and exquisite to the touch!

Clear, easy-on-the-eye type makes reading a pleasure again! These are stories to be enjoyed. And owning them shows your appreciation of fine books.

Clue #3—Fabulous FREE Book. Fabulous FREE Read!

Get *The New Bedside, Bathtub & Armchair Companion to Agatha Christie* as your FREE GIFT just for previewing *The Agatha Christie Mystery Collection*. Over 360 pages filled with story plots (but *never* the endings!), photos, facts about Agatha's life, and the many movies and plays of her work. This $12.95 value is yours to keep *absolutely free*, no matter what!

You also get *And Then There Were None* free for 15 days to read and enjoy. Here's your chance to sample *The Agatha Christie Mystery Collection* without risk—enjoy this classic "whodunit," then decide for yourself if you wish to keep it.

No Obligation—EVER!

It all adds up! Send for your no-risk preview of *And Then There Were None*. Enjoy it *free* for 15 days! We'll send your Agatha Christie *Companion* free, and start your *Agatha Christie Mystery Collection* right away. Each volume in the Collection arrives with the same *free 15 day preview*. *No* minimum number of books to buy. No obligation. *You may cancel at any time!* Mail the reply card today!

The Solution Is Easy!

1. Try the *Agatha Christie Mystery Collection* without risk! Complete the picture on the reply card below (Hint: the missing piece is on the front page of this offer!), then return the card to us and you'll receive *And Then There Were None* to read and enjoy for 15 days FREE!

2. You get *The New Bedside, Bathtub & Armchair Companion to Agatha Christie* FREE when you do! It's yours to keep even if you cancel your membership. Now you have all the facts! Mail the Reply Card Today!

Don't resist our splendid offer! Send for your *free preview* of Agatha Christie's classic *And Then There Were None*, PLUS get your 363-page Agatha Christie *Bedside Companion* FREE! See details inside.

five eldest sons of the men who had sponsored Sarah Bernstein. The first four were dead. According to the late Freddy Marchand, Mr. Turner, Jr. now stood to inherit over a million dollars. Spencer rang the bell and waited.

Chapter 20

A confrontation with the fifth son.

Spencer heard a click, and a tiny window of stained glass set inside the door opened. A shaft of light flooded out, then an eye filled the square.

"Yes?"

"Mr. Turner?"

"Yes. What do you want?"

"My name is Spencer Holmes. I am a private detective. I have been hired to investigate the murder of a young man on the very cusp of his marriage to Felicity Harrington. There have been four more victims since then, all of whom are connected, and with whom you are acquainted. The fourth, Frederick Marchand, met his death this evening at a performance of the opera which you attended. I had the criminal in my hands. He was about your height."

There was a pause. Spencer continued.

"May I come in?"

"Do you have any identification?"

"See here, my good man. I am proud to live in a democratic society where the guilty are considered innocent until the last possible moment. But your time is rapidly running out. There is a good deal of evidence against you. I know about the will. You had motive and, this evening at least, opportunity. If I call the police you will be arrested immediately. The only reason I have refrained from doing so is that I prefer the symmetry of completing a case myself. And if you think you will make another spectacular exit, you are quite mistaken. There are no innocent bystanders here to subdue my actions. I have several men surrounding the property who are under orders to block your escape with any means necessary. Now, there is to be no more shilly-shallying! Open this door!"

The speech had its intended effect, orchestrated as it had

been on a rising note of anger. Yet the man still refused to allow Spencer inside.

"All right, all right. Hold on a moment. I'm going to check your credentials. I'll be right back."

Footsteps faded away. Spencer stepped up on the welcome mat and peered through the little window Turner had left open. He could see an elegant hallway, beige walls hung with expensive Spanish paintings. He heard the man make a phone call. He heard his own name, then silence as the man listened. Finally the receiver was replaced and Turner came back to the door. Spencer heard the chain lifted, then a dead bolt shot open and the door swung inward.

"You are—?" Spencer was astounded.

"Of course."

The man in front of him was not the height of his recent opponent, but a good deal shorter and a great deal rounder. Apparently he had been standing on tiptoe to bring his eye level with the peephole, and Spencer now realized that he himself had been standing on a lower step. The man weighed close to three hundred pounds and was almost perfectly spheroid, which considerably compromised his ability to leap across a wide, empty space. Spencer tried once more to bring the salient facts to a logical conclusion.

"Mr. Stephen Douglas Turner, Jr? The son of Mr. Stephen Douglas Turner, the attorney?"

"Yes, yes. I'm the man you want. I'm the fifth. Come in."

The man waddled down the hall and into a living room plushly furnished in leather and glass. A wide picture window looked over the bay.

"That was a friend of mine from the district attorney's office. He knew your name and described you. You will excuse me, I hope, but I am sure you can appreciate how frightened I am. Until this moment, I was unaware Frederick had been killed. It's true, I'm the last one alive now. Why don't we sit down?" He pointed to a sofa. Spencer took a seat, keeping a wary eye on the rotund man.

Turner sat opposite him in a brown leather armchair. The man pressed his fingers together, forming a steeple, and peered over at Spencer with small, rabbit eyes.

"Mr. Holmes, what am I to do?"

Chapter 21

A lengthy conversation fails to bring the case to its expected climax.

This was a question Spencer had not anticipated. Events had unfolded rapidly and the discovery of the tontine trust had provided the neccessary motivation. Four men, connected only by an inheritance, had been murdered. Spencer had arrived at the doorstep of the fifth with the full momentum of a complete theory. Now it appeared there were undiscovered elements yet to be unearthed. Spencer was anxious to address the problem, but first felt compelled to face Turner's situation directly.

"You might hire bodyguards."

"Would that have prevented Robert Hansen from suffering a heart attack?"

"Probably not. You might go on a long ocean voyage."

"I have recently returned from a long ocean voyage. When I arrived home, I found the obituary notices of Fleischakel, Pearl, and Hansen on my desk, along with the newspaper report of the unfortunate young man who was shot on his wedding day. My clipping service forwards to me anything concerning my clients. Now you tell me they, and Marchand tonight, were murdered. It does seem overly coincidental, but are you absolutely sure these events are connected?"

"I found a witness who was present at the murder of Harry Pearl. Mr. Fleischakel could not have drowned in his own grapes; it is altogether too unlikely. The death of Mr. Hansen was indeed massive interruption of his coronary muscles, but it was induced by drug, a derivative of digitalis, delivered in a tiny frozen dart, probably propelled from some form of a blowgun. The coroner will find only a tiny pinprick in the side of the neck, which could have been caused shaving. Squill starts the heart fibrillating; too much of it can easily kill a man, much less a sixty-five-year-old with a rapidly beating heart. I confronted

Marchand earlier this evening, and provided him with a body-guard who was subsequently knocked unconscious. Mar-chand's death was meant to look like he accidentally got caught in the rope system and hung himself, but the coroner will eventually find that he had been overcome by a blow to the head before strangulation was induced."

"It does seem overly coincidental. The question is, who could be doing this?"

"You could. The ocean voyage and your appearance in the audience tonight could be calculated, preplanned alibis, and do not preclude the fact that you might have hired a confederate to carry out the murders. This apartment is not inexpensive. You have resources."

Turner thought this over glumly, then looked straight at Spencer.

"I suppose you will investigate, regardless of what I say. Well, I hope you do. I hope you find something. I seem to be in a precarious position."

"Do you have any relatives who might inherit your money after you gained it?"

"No. I'm an only child. Both my parents are dead. I have left my entire estate to a number of charities. I hardly think the YMCA could engineer such a coup."

"About this trust, can you explain it in more detail?"

"Yes, of course. I helped draw it up. I am the executor. I'm an attorney, you see, as my father was. We had an office together until he died."

"Were you aware of the . . . unusual circumstances?"

"I knew about their mistress and her daughter, if that's what you mean. The murders make a good deal of sense, now that I think about it. How old is the daughter?"

"Just twenty-one."

"Yes, right. Well, my father and his friends left her $20,000 apiece. She was to—"

"The men left *her* the money—not the sons?"

"Well, she was to receive it on her twenty-first birthday with one provision: that she be married by that time. I suppose that explains the unfortunate boy's termination."

"I *thought* he was an innocent. The murder and her impending birthday were all too convenient. Why the unusual codicil?"

"That's easy. Just consider the era in which these men lived. They were Victorians with Victorian morals. To them, an unmarried woman was a dishonest one. It didn't stop them from a relationship with Sarah Bernstein. A mistress was considered quite proper, especially at their age. But they had no intention of encouraging such behavior in their daughter. It was a sort of guarantee that they would not be subsidizing another . . . loose woman. She was to be either married or disinherited before her majority."

"But she didn't know this?"

"No, they didn't want her to engage in a marriage of convenience. Also, she was adopted if you remember, and had no knowledge of her unusual parentage. Our office kept track of her secretly, and was prepared to turn over the money."

"Now that she's twenty-one, and not yet married, she loses the money?"

"That's right. The trust becomes a tontine, which you seem to know something about."

"A great deal of money now goes to the last surviving firstborn son."

"That's right. A tontine trust is fairly unusual, except when one party gets the income for life and then the capital goes elsewhere on that party's death. That's really what it's for. In this case the fund remained intact, which is why the amount built up so heavily."

"Who controls it?"

"The Bank of America Trust Department. I get an annual report as executor."

"Why did your father participate in such an odd scheme?"

"Well, it was a sort of lottery. You see, the five men never knew which of them was the actual father. So they decided on the tontine as a way of settling the money, in case it didn't go to the girl, on one of their sons at random. All of them were wealthy, and there was plenty more to go around. My father left me a substantial estate. The tontine represented only the $20,000 they'd contributed to the Bernstein fund. Actually, they all probably thought the girl would collect."

"Everything makes sense. When the boy was murdered, the

girl was no longer eligible to collect. And since each son has died, leaving only you, the inheritance becomes yours. Which places you in a most suspicious position."

Turner rose and walked to the window. He gazed out at the numerous twinkling lights across the bay and the running lights on ships cruising the night seas. He turned back to Spencer.

"Mr. Holmes, my friend at the district attorney's office did more than confirm your honest reputation as a private detective. He spoke of you as a formidable man. I understand my position. I will give you access to any information regarding my life you request. I did not murder any of these people."

Spencer had in the past been offered similar challenges. Many evil men were driven by a need to demonstrate their own invincibility by taunting their pursuers. That compulsion to play the game at the very edge of danger characterized men on both sides of law and order. He would follow through on this case whether or not it led to Stephen Douglas Turner, Jr.

Turner spoke with increasing passion.

"I did not kill anyone. Under the circumstances you can understand why I am becoming uneasy. Perhaps out there somewhere, there is a murderous altruist who wants to see the money settled on the Boy Scouts and the YMCA. If so, I too am in danger. Someone is killing the sons of the Weekday Club."

Spencer certainly knew this. He scrutinized Turner, who only stared morosely at his own feet. Then Spencer turned to stare idly out at the midnight sea. There had to be another reason four adults and a young man about to become their half-brother-in-law had been slain. Spencer would find out what it was. In the meantime, he would offer Mr. Turner what little advice he could.

"There are two men watching this building. They are from the Pinkerton detective agency. I will see that they remain here throughout the night. Tomorrow morning you'll have to make your own arrangements."

"Thank you. I'll do that."

"Just a few more things. If all five of you have inherited substantial estates, what happened to the money inherited by Pearl and Marchand? Pearl was working as a manager of a topless bar and Marchand was a stagehand."

"Harry Pearl wanted to prove he could do without his father's money or help. There was a lot of competition between father and son. He wouldn't take any money or listen to his father on anything. So old man Perlmutter left most everything to a daughter. Marchand got a substantial sum from Carl, but lost it all in the stock market. He was a heavy gambler."

"How long have you been out of the United States?"

"Three months. I went all over the South Pacific."

"What happens to the money if you die?"

"That depends on the judge. The strictest interpretation is that as the last survivor, I receive the money. It would be added to my estate and go to the charities I named. The girl could get a good lawyer and try to argue that the intent of the trust was for her to receive the money and the marriage-by-twenty-one provision was an irrational, incompetent act. It would be a tough case to prove. My father drew up all five wills for the men, as well as constructing the trust. I would say the trust is perfectly sound."

"An outsider could not put their hands on the money?"

"I suppose an officer at the bank could embezzle it, but insurance would cover that. Now that I'm the last survivor, I could change my will before something happens to me."

With that thought Turner's face darkened and he moved away from the window.

"How much did you have to do with the other four sons?"

"Very little. We were neither friends nor business associates like our fathers. My firm handled their fathers' legal affairs, and as the old men passed away, we probated their estates. That's about all."

"Who else knows about the mistress and the money?"

"That's hard to say. Five different men, each with their own circle of acquaintances. They could have told anyone, or no one. It would seem like pretty confidential information."

"Yes. Your mother, for instance. She didn't know?"

"No, I don't think so. Certainly not in detail. Father was a real family man, except on Mondays. For twenty-five years I thought that was his bowling night. A couple of years before he died he explained about the girl and her daughter, and I helped him draw up the trust."

For a moment both men took the measure of the other. Then Spencer rose.

"Thank you. I must go. I have a great deal to think about. I will be in touch."

They walked to the door. Spencer left him with a short warning.

"We are, none of us, above suspicion."

Spencer left the house with his own suspicions still unclear. The last several days had been notable for the lies he had encountered, but how many, and by whom, he could not put his finger on. A vague feeling of uneasiness accompanied him back to the mansion.

After Spencer had gone, Turner locked and bolted the door. He walked around the apartment, checking that all the windows were secured, then turned on the burglar alarm system. He went back to the front door and drew the curtains across the window. For a few moments, he sat in the armchair, brooding. It was nearly one A.M. when he went to the bar, poured himself a stiff drink, and returned to his favorite chair. He took a sip of expensive Scotch whiskey and put the glass on a table near his hand. An expression, at once full of surprise and fear, flitted briefly across his face. Then his chin fell to his chest.

The fifth and last firstborn son of the benefactors of Ms. Sarah Bernstein was dead.

Part III

Chapter 1

Recriminations.

"The murderer," spoke Spencer sadly, "has been ahead of us at every step."

An early edition of the *Chronicle* had brought the news of Turner's demise.

Spencer and Mr. Dihje were seated on a small terrace outside the kitchen. African roses in planter boxes made a low fence on three sides. The glass tabletop held the remains of eggs Mandarin, and a striped beach umbrella threw a circle of shade on the two men. Spencer took a sip of his espresso; Mr. Dihje warmed his hands on a mug of herbal tea. Both digested their eggs and Spencer's statement.

"Six deaths. Inexplicably related." Spencer continued with his verbal ramble. "The cold-blooded and calculated murder of a young man over whom our operatives can discover not a shadow of the nefarious. This prevents Felicity Harrington, née Bernstein, from engaging in the ancient and noble institution of marriage . . . and just prior to her twenty-first birthday, when she would have, unexpectedly, received a million-dollar trust fund . . . from five men, all of whom believed themselves to be her natural father. The money is then to settle upon the last surviving firstborn son of the five men, each of whom meets his death under accidental circumstances in too rapid succession to be believable. In fact, we can be assured they were the victims of exceedingly clever foul play. The money now goes to Christian charities. . . . In short, we seem to have returned to the beginning. We are without motive, means, or opportunity."

Finally, thinking of his grandfather's most famous theorem, he ended on a dark note. "Not only has the impossible been eliminated, but the improbable as well."

Spencer sighed.

A sea gull wheeled across their view. Spencer tossed a crust of seven-grain toast into the air and watched the great bird intercept the crumb in a calculated arc. So graceful, Spencer thought. The truly brilliant criminal mind was graceful. In action, so swift and clever. All those calculations, precautions, maneuvers that were necessary to enact six murders. The criminal mind, while being despised for its morality, may be admired for its complexity.

The doorbell interrupted his rambling interior monologue.

"Fate," Spencer said aloud to Mr. Dihje, "sometimes knocks right at the front door. Please usher whoever is knocking at ours, in."

Chapter 2

A brief appearance of the regular forces.

Shareen Kelly, chief of the five-man Belvedere police department, joined Spencer on the terrace. Mr. Dihje withdrew discreetly, leaving them alone. Since it was unlike Mr. Dihje to absent himself from a conversation that might bear on a case under investigation, his departure was startling to Spencer.

Among the women of Spencer's acquaintance, Chief Kelly was numbered as, if not the most beautiful, certainly the most striking. She was, at six feet, almost as tall as he. She possessed athletic grace, and had come onto the terrace with impatient ease, hard on Mr. Dihje's heels. She had luxuriant and natural red hair. Her occupation coincided with Spencer's principal interest.

Mr. Dihje knew all this, and, long anxious to see a woman's touch applied to a few of the more haphazard routines of the household, had purposely swallowed his curiosity to leave them alone on the patio.

What Mr. Dihje didn't know is that Spencer, in almost every other aspect a man of the modern world, found himself to be ill at ease with aggressive women. As much as he believed in the equality of the sexes and in women's rights, he was, in some unfathomable depth of his psyche, unable to translate that intellectual understanding into appropriate behavior. He yearned to. But when they approached him, or the reverse, in even the most businesslike of circumstances, he found himself admiring their legs, or their breasts, or their soft, lovely faces, as much as or more than their words. Chief Kelly, who had been a feature of the Bay area's police force for some years now, had especially impressed him in the looks department, an admirer as he was of the physically fit and strong-featured female.

He stood up and indicated a vacant chair in what he hoped was a gracious, and not condescending, manner.

Kelly opened the conversation with reluctance.

"We're stuck."

It was a rare occasion when any of the department's finest made such an admission. The female of the species in particular.

"You are speaking of the Harrington wedding case, I presume."

Chief Kelly frowned. "It's the principal topic of conversation in the papers. What case are *you* working on?"

"The same. Speaking of the newspapers, I noticed your organization expects to make an arrest soon, according to the commissioner. May I take it that he is jumping the gun on the men in the trenches somewhat?"

"We've gotten exactly nowhere. The commissioner is a blowhard and a politician."

"That's redundant. So, though loath I am to admit it, have I."

"Nonsense. You've been investigating for a week. And Harrington has given you carte blanche. Let's have it, Spencer."

"Your confidence in my ability is most flattering, but really, it is not my intention to hold out on the police force. Besides, you know I'm putty in your hands."

Spencer hoped his last remark might go overlooked, as it was so wide of the truth as to be termed a howler. He simply had no ability for small talk. He tried again.

"I have been attempting to bring the motive to light. I found a financial connection with a group of men who stood to inherit a large sum of money because the bride remains unmarried."

"You think the murder was meant to prevent the marriage? That's a little farfetched, isn't it? And talk about a photo finish."

"Exactly what I think. Murder is seldom carried out in front of an audience. Why plan the most difficult course when so many others are available? The dark alley, the house at night, the lonely road—all of these are so much more convenient. No, it seems to me that someone waited until the last minute, perhaps in the hope of avoiding the deed altogether. That indicates the significance of the ceremony."

"A lot of money is a terrific motive. Who are these men?"

"Were, I'm afraid. They are all recently deceased."

"Hell. Then you really are stuck too?"

"I am regrouping. There is still much to investigate."

"What's the story on these men?"

The story, as Spencer had gathered it so far, was incomplete. And he had a legally defined relationship of confidentiality with a client. Spencer spoke cautiously.

"They were the beneficiaries of the money. The San Francisco police department has logged four of their deaths as accidental. A heart attack, a convulsion, and two industrial accidents. The Sonoma sheriff's department adds a drowning to the list."

"What happens to the money?"

"It goes to charity."

Kelly thought about it for all of several seconds.

"This isn't very promising, Spencer. Five accidental deaths."

"I am convinced there is ample evidence of foul play."

"In all five?"

"Yes."

"What's the motive?"

"I haven't one as yet."

"What's the connection if not the money?"

"I do not know."

Kelly thought this over. Then she said, "People die all the time."

"May I quote you?"

"You know perfectly well what I mean. There are accidents all the time. Twenty-two-and-a-half people die of natural causes every day in San Francisco alone. How old were they?"

"All middle-approaching-late age."

"And nothing connected them?"

"Their fathers were in business together. Some twenty years ago, however."

"And Harrington is paying you for this investigation?"

"Do I detect a small but calculated note of envy of the private sector?"

"All right. Let's leave it alone. You don't have anything else to fork over?"

"Does the police academy provide you with these colorful expressions?"

Kelly smiled. It was the piece de résistance of her natural

beauty. "I can't help it. I guess I read Mickey Spillane too much. Anyway, the fact is, I was in the neighborhood on another matter and thought I ought to drop by, since we're working on the same case. It's good to see you."

"It's good to see you." Not very original, but true, and the best Spencer could respond with at the moment. He always felt that something was left unsaid between him and this lovely and talented woman, but he was never sure what it was. Or how to say it.

She stood up. "Well, I better go. We've got a packetful of information coming back from Washington."

"Don't you have something to tell me?"

"What do you mean?"

"My dear Chief Kelly. I am not in the habit of passing out information for the use of your department because I am a citizen with a sense of social responsibility. Have you never seen a movie or television show or read a book about cops and robbers? The public detectives and the private investigators, when not taking a belligerent stance, share a certain relationship which usually undertakes to deliver a quid pro quo. Fork, as you say, it over."

"You think what you gave me was information? I call it the bum's rush."

"It is, all the same, all that I have in the nature of suspicion. If I had any concrete evidence I would have brought it up."

She sat down.

"Well, it won't hurt to tell you," she said.

"The fact is," Spencer said as kindly as he could, "that Harrington has passed on to you, through your superiors, the request—though considering his influence it might just as well be termed an order—that you share with me any and all information on the case arising from your investigations. And you have come here to satisfy that request. Am I not correct?"

"He told you?"

"He didn't have to. That is the way he operates. I might add that while he does not wish to convey any lack of confidence in the police department—I believe he is a regular subscriber to the annual ball—he does place the utmost trust in me. I still hope to prove it justified. So. What's the scoop?"

Kelly postponed the moment of her humiliation by taking

her time extracting a notebook from her black patent-leather purse. While she did so, Spencer kept the conversation alive.

"Are you wearing what is described in your business as plain clothes?"

"Yes, why?" She was immediately suspicious.

"Oh, it's lovely. Don't take this amiss. But your purse. It's practically army issue. It gives you away as surely as brown shoes and white socks do your male comrades. You know, Gucci is doing some wonderful things these days."

"When did you become a fashion expert?"

"Forgive me. It was none of my business."

Kelly had her notebook out, and whether or not by design, placed her purse out of sight under the chair. She flipped open the black leather book.

"The bullet was 6.5 millimeter, from a rifle. It penetrated and lodged into the rear right cranium, causing death instantaneously. Given the angle of entry, the shot had to be fired from the crowd, the house, or the trees or ground beyond—anywhere on the right or right rear of the victim. We haven't—"

"One moment. If the shot was fired from the estate, how did the murderer effect his entrance and exit so easily? Unless it was a guest, which is also highly unlikely, given the number of available witnesses."

"We haven't discovered that yet."

"I might suggest another theory."

"Yes?"

"The shot was fired from the bay side. On the groom's left."

"But the angle of entry—"

"—is correct. However, the testimony of the maid of honor tells us that the groom had in fact turned away from the priest and settled his idolatrous gaze on his beloved."

Kelly tried to picture this in her mind. "You think the assassin was in the crowd on the *groom's* side of the altar?"

"Or beyond."

"Beyond the crowd on that side there are sheer, inaccessible cliffs. Beyond the cliffs is the open bay."

"Correct."

"Impossible."

"Perhaps. Perhaps not."

"Short of a large conspiracy, the killer couldn't have been in the crowd, not with a weapon as large as a rifle. He couldn't have gotten in or out of those cliffs without being seen. And you can't fire a shot from a boat that far away and expect to hit the broad side of a thirty-two room mansion, much less the cranium of a human being. The killer had to be on the estate side of the crowd. He got away through the house perhaps, or over the walls behind it."

"That is an alternate theory, I admit."

Kelly looked suspiciously at Spencer for a moment. She frowned and tugged at her earlobe. Then she shrugged.

"Anyway, we haven't found the weapon yet, but it's got to be on the grounds somewhere. My men are still searching. We're combing the trees for signs of climbing and searching for the bullet shell throughout the area. Nothing has turned up yet. We forwarded the fingerprints of every person present to Washington; the results should arrive any hour now."

"It was a very highbrow guest list."

"Yeah. But you never know. We did the servants too. I don't expect much. Four hundred people can trample the grass pretty well; there were too many footprints on the lawn and none on the grounds. I have four men investigating the boy. He was a student at Berkeley. As a precaution, two of them are undercover. Frankly, that's where I expect a break. There or on the streets. We've put the heat on every informer we have."

"Surely you don't think—"

"Thinking is your privilege, Spencer. I'm paid to investigate. That means a systematic follow-up on every lead, real or not. Last night we checked out a woman who telephoned Harrington to say that his future son-in-law's fate had been written in the stars."

"Colorful job, yours."

"You never know what will turn up. She was growing marijuana in her solarium."

"And you cited her?" Spencer, an infrequent but grateful devotee of that particular species of weed, was astonished. "In San Francisco?"

"Every collar helps. We weren't all born rich."

The silence this time was mutual. A definite depression, due to the appalling lack of physical evidence, set in. Though neither acknowledged it, both had expected the other to till more fertile ground. Finally Kelly rose again and headed for the door. Mr. Dihje appeared as if by magic to lead the way. Spencer followed in his dressing gown and slippers.

When they reached the front door, Kelly turned.

"If there's anything worthwhile in the FBI package, I'll send a copy over."

"There won't be."

"No." Even Kelly couldn't envision that. But she brightened. "Well, so long. I'll let you know when we break the case."

"I will hold my breath."

And on that little trading of satire, the party broke up.

Immediately after the door closed between Kelly and him, Spencer shed his previous mood of torpor. He fairly bounded for the stairs.

"Mr. Dihje, we mustn't let the grass grow under our feet. We will be quite active now, I believe. We have any number of stops to make."

"We investigate?"

"Indeed we do. We investigate, we ferret out, we run down, we may even snoop. We shall begin with the deceased. One always knows where to find them."

Inside of half an hour, the dynamic duo were speeding down Post Street in their little beige Beetle.

Chapter 3

In which the deceased has little to say.

At their first stop, death was everywhere. It was the city morgue, and as Spencer had spent many an enjoyable hour there studying the characteristics of the human body, he was a welcome visitor among the members of the coroner's office. He was admired for any number of his own contributions, as well as his ability, rare among the staff members' outside acquaintances, to share a certain ghoulish, professional humor. ("Any *body* home?" he had asked on his arrival, then chuckled aloud.) Mr. Dihje also was welcome, for a large proportion of the staff shared his Eastern heritage.

Today the two men stood with three others around a stainless-steel table which might have groaned, if it could, under the weight of Mr. Turner, recently of Telegraph Hill. His face was waxen, his skin clammy and cold to the touch. His flesh spilled copiously over the sides but also modestly hid his private parts.

"An unusual but not overly rare case," said the medical examiner in his professional tone. "A seizure of the nervous system causing the heart valves to close and the lung to cease respirating. Epileptics may occasionally suffer this if their convulsions are strong enough. A kind of sensory overload."

"This man was not an epileptic, however."

"That's right. His own doctor was here this morning and confirmed that. Of course, it can happen to anyone."

"What causes the nervous system to seize?"

"We don't really know. Too much pain can be one way. Torture victims sometimes suffer it. The individual blows, or pain inflicted, might not be expected to kill the person, but cumulatively it becomes too much. The nervous system revolts, blocking off the pain. It doesn't, of course, have any awareness that by shutting down, its owner will be unable to breathe or fibrillate."

"No sign here of anything of that nature?"

"Oh, no. You can see there isn't a mark on the body. Not even a burn. Electrocution is another possible cause, but in this case there is no sign of that either. This was a defect in the nervous system, I'm afraid. Perhaps genetically programmed from birth, like a bad heart."

"Or engineered chemically."

"Well, I don't know of any chemical that might have that effect. We did a complete chemical analysis of the blood as soon as you phoned. Here's the breakdown."

The quartet moved to a counter at the side and Dr. Terrence Michaels, M.E., punched up some figures on the screen. They all studied them quietly for a while.

"Hmmm. The curious case of alcohol in the bloodstream," murmured Spencer.

The doctor was puzzled.

"But there isn't a trace of alcohol in the bloodstream, Mr. Holmes.

"That," Spencer pronounced triumphantly, unable to contain his glee at having trapped the man into the straight line he had hoped for, "is what is so curious. There should be. There was a tumbler of pure Scotch at his elbow when he died. The police report makes that quite clear."

"Maybe he didn't have a chance to drink it?"

"Or maybe the first small sip was enough to kill him. A pity the police had no suspicion of foul play."

"What could be so powerful?"

"Curare. Especially as prepared by certain tribes of South America. Just a drop of it on the end of a dart can bring down an elephant."

"In the drink?"

"Nothing more efficient. It's odorless and tasteless and colorless. The victim would never know, certainly not be forewarned. Can you scan for any other foreign chemicals?"

"Yes." Dr. Michaels tapped half a dozen more buttons on the computer and the machine whirred. A list of mathematical formulae appeared on the screen. "Here's something. $C_{58}H_4xC_{12}N_2O_{65}H_2O$. Now what the hell is that?"

His assistant immediately pulled down a heavy black book

entitled *Known Chemical Substances* and began to flip through the pages.

"Don't bother, Mr. Wong. You are looking at the algebraic expression for dried extract of the woody vine *Strychnos Tox-ifera*. Filtered of impurities over a simple camp fire, it becomes the principal weapon of the feared and powerful pygmies." Spencer now turned to his own assistant. "I think it is confirmed, then. Six murders, Mr. Dihje. The man we seek is knowledgeable and well-traveled. And deadly. We had better be off. Thank you for your trouble, doctor."

As they walked past the voluminous flesh of Turner, the doctor glanced down.

"What should I put on the death certificate, Mr. Holmes?"

"The sins of our fathers, Dr. Michaels."

Chapter 4

Further investigation into the recent life of Mr. Turner.

"Our next stop will be the Telegraph Hill apartment of the dear departed," Spencer said, somewhat in the manner of a tour guide. "We need to know more about this man. I suspect he was the most intelligent of the lot, and he alone seems to have known the full details of the Weekday Club, stemming, I assume, from his involvement with the legal affairs of his father and his father's business associates."

The car sidled into a parking space on the steep hill and Spencer prudently turned the wheel against the curb. He retraced his steps of the night before, with Mr. Dihje at his heels. The front door featured a wide adhesive band with the words "No entry, Police Department" printed in red. Spencer stepped aside and Mr. Dihje, employing his thin, flat stiletto, neatly separated the warning from the door. He spent a few seconds on the lock, and then swung the door open and stood aside for Spencer to resume the lead.

The apartment was almost as Spencer had seen it the night before. Apparently the maid, who had discovered the deceased, sensed that her weekly stipend for cleaning the establishment would not be forthcoming, and had decided to skip her customary routine. Even Mr. Turner's After Six jacket lay where he had tossed it. Spencer felt for a wallet and was rewarded. He went through it methodically.

"Driver's license. Social Security. Blue Cross. San Francisco Bar Association. Nothing unusual in all that. Well, well, an amateur member of a noble fraternity: he was a member of the Dashiell Hammett fan club. They meet irregularly in the second-floor room of John's Bar and Grill, I believe. Credit cards; no help there—they're practically given away. A chess club in North Beach. Of course, I should have noticed the Vienna gambit in place on the board there. I say, he was a grand master. His hobbies dovetail, at any rate. A logical mind, and passionless. Let's take a look at his library. The fingerprints of the mind never lie."

They strolled down a hall and turned into a well-furnished study, one wall of which was lined with books. Spencer ran his hands over them lovingly, with the practical respect of the ardent bibliophile.

"Famous criminal cases. Not unlikely for an attorney, except our man's practice was principally estates and contracts, and not criminal, or I would have seen him around the dockets. Travel guides. A principal activity. Plenty of mysteries in fine editions. Yes, here are all the Hammett books. And the English are well represented. The Watson accounts of my grandfather. I am mollified. Marsh . . . Innes . . . Crispin . . . Excellent collection. A preponderance of locked-room mysteries. Fascinating. No hint of poisons. I think we can rule out suicide, even if he did feel my own hot breath upon his conscience. Coffeetable art . . . Hemingway . . . that would satisfy the unfulfilled need for machismo. The paradox of the well-to-do: life is simply too easy for them. It frustrates our basic instincts to fight for survival. Let's see where his more recent concerns lay."

They penetrated farther along the hall and landed in the bachelor's inner sanctum, dominated by a double bed, not slept in recently. Several books and magazines were piled on a night table. An open suitcase was laying at the foot of the bed.

"Look here, the laundry has all been removed, but the clean clothes are still in place. As is the toilet kit. I believe our man was intending another trip. And on the very heels of his return from a long cruise. Interesting."

Spencer stood over the table.

"His most recent concerns. DISTINCTIVE HOMES. I wonder if he was planning a move up in the world? And Christie's *Murder on the Orient Express*. Very illuminating. Let's see if our man had any secrets."

Spencer stepped to the cabinet beneath the table and opened it.

"What, no pornography? Not even a copy of *The Joy of Sex*. A celibate bachelor, or one of simple tastes, at any rate. Too bad. The darker recesses of a man's soul nearly always reveal a clue to a hidden ambition or two. Ah well, I think we've learned a great deal, don't you? And tempus fugit. Let's be off; we return to the hallways of the dead."

Chapter 5

Wherein we observe the tedious research which forms the principal portion of modern detective work.

The morgue they arrived at this time was a repository of the deed, not the flesh. They stood among endless rows of drawers containing microfilmed editions of the *San Francisco Chronicle,* and filing cabinets brimming with clippings. Spencer sketched out an outline of their approach.

"What we need to do is compile an account of the Weekday Club. The principal activities of our five satyrs. In particular, anything that may have connected them—except Miss Bernstein, of course. It is unlikely they allowed anything of that particular endeavor to find its way into the society columns. You take Hansen and Marchand, I'll start with Turner and Perlmutter. Fleischakel spent most of his time in Napa Valley so there will be less on him. Happy hunting."

Their tomb of information was musty, dusty, and silent. For several hours, not a word passed between them. Both took copious notes and scrambled back and forth between the files and the microfilm, cross-checking references. Their job was made simpler by the wealth and notoriety of the five men.

At last Spencer gathered up his notes.

"Lunchtime, I think. I do so hate the tedious research of this job. It is exhausting and completely glossed over in glamorous fictional accounts."

Mr. Dihje made a few final marks on his pad and put the papers in front of him in order. They rose together and walked toward the exit.

"Let's dine at John's," Spencer said when they reached the street. "They have an excellent five-pound steak, if I'm not mistaken."

Research being as boring for the reader as it is for the gumshoe, we too shall skip over the lengthy results of the long, back-aching, eye-straining morning and repair with them to a light repast at the excellent bar and grill at 63 Ellis Street.

Chapter 6

A hard-boiled meal.

Swing open the glass doors of this ancient eatery and you enter the all-too-rare world of the unpretentious. In these days of theme restaurants, where one can visit a Victorian railway car, safari to Africa, kick the dust off one's boots in a wild West saloon, or dine in the plastic-decor world of Mildred Pierce, what a relief it is to eat and drink without the distraction of a Hollywood set. How Sam Spade would ever have enjoyed a meal that began with the necessity of choosing between one hundred different versions of the hamburger, how Nick and Nora Charles's famished terrier would have survived on table scraps from a nouvelle cuisine meal, how Philip Marlowe would have plied information from a contact over a San Pellegrino, is beyond imagination.

Yet here such a man still feels safe from haute cuisine and delicate decor. Here the necessity of transferring the fork to the right hand before bringing the working end to one's mouth might go overlooked without worry. Here the small pool of coffee floating in the saucer beneath the cup would not be considered gauche.

At the long bar, serviced by a man who clearly does not spend his evenings in leather and his vacations in Key West, one can perch on a leather stool simply to engage in serious drinking. One can knock back a few doubles without being taken for a weak personality. One might order "eggs" or "steak" or, even, "steak and eggs," with no more qualifications than "over" and "rare." The potatoes are never sculpted. The coffee is black.

It was to this restaurant that Spencer Holmes and Mr. Dihje retreated from their long morning in the newspaper morgue. Spencer ordered a martini and a steak. Mr. Dihje was satisfied with a salad. (With good reason. It might be noted that since arriving in the land of cornucopian abundance he had added to his small figure a spare tire, and had only this morning committed himself to a series of less prodigious meals.) There were no specials. The waiter mercifully described nothing. He took their order with neither impoliteness nor strained frivolity, and left.

While awaiting their food, Spencer and Mr. Dihje compared notes. Several years of close companionship allowed them to communicate with a minimum of language. The occasional need for privacy in public places had added a layer of impenetrable shorthand. For these reasons, it would be fruitless of us to attempt to overhear their conversation. The results, however, were outlined by Spencer for insertion in his growing file on the case, and would have been recorded in something like the following manner.

The Weekday Club:

1. HAROLD FLEISCHAKEL b. San Francisco, 1895. d. 1975. m. Irene Rothman, 1935. One son, Randal, two daughters, Celia and Marie. Founder and owner, Essex Vintners. Member, Winemakers Association of Northern California, President, 1954–59. Grad: University of Washington. Member: Bohemian Club. Winner, Prix de France for a '65 Burgundy. Hobbies: rowing, stamp collecting. Board of Directors: Arco Mines, Marin Tennis Club, Napa Valley Board of Education. Army, 1914–18.

2. CARL MARCHAND b. San Francisco, 1896. d. 1969. m. Marie Leighton, 1923. One son, Frederick, one daughter, Leigh. Founder, Marchand department stores. Member, American Retailers Association, President, 1955–56. Grad: New York University. Member: Bohemian Club. Retired, 1965, sold Marchand's to Retail Associates chain. Hobbies: music, writing. Board of Directors: San Francisco Opera, Marin Tennis Club, Retail Associates, San Francisco Conservatory of Music. Army, 1914–18.

3. STEPHEN DOUGLAS TURNER b. San Francisco, 1895. d. 1979. m. Virginia Worthman, 1925. One son, Stephen, Jr. Founding partner, Turner, Bachman and Turner. Appointed judgeship to Superior Court, 1945. Grad: University of San Francisco and U.S.F law school. Member: American Bar Association, President, 1961–63, Bohemian Club. Hobbies: astronomy, sailing. Board of Directors: Marin Tennis Club, Stan-

dard Oil of California, Bank of America. Board of Regents, U.S.F. Army: 1914–18.

4. ROBERT PERLMUTTER b. San Francisco, 1892. d. 1967. m. Arlene Skolsky, 1926. One son, Harris. Raised in Hebrew Orphanage. Founder Allred Taxi Fleet of San Francisco. Member: Bohemian Club. Hobbies: tennis, golf. Board of Directors: American Transportation Union, Marin Tennis Club. Army: 1914–18.

5. WILLIAM HANSEN b. San Francisco, 1898. d. 1969. m. Shirley Rhyder, 1938. Twin children, Robert and Barbara. Successful jockey, 1926–41. Owner, Hansen Ranch in Danville. Breeder of thoroughbreds, including Soft Ride, 1959 best overall performance. Member: Jockeys Association, President, 1932–38, Bohemian Club. Hobbies: hunting, fishing. Board of Directors: Calumet Farms, Marin Tennis Club. Army: 1914–18.

All of this was available in the obituary files, and much of it had been taken from a Who's Who entry by a reporter with no time to unearth facts himself. A number of related articles were dug out of back issues by diligent cross-referencing. These culminated in an abstract listing of assorted facts along the following lines.

1. Their unit of the Sixth Army had landed in Italy prior to the invasion, and slogged its way north for months of bitter fighting, during which Fleischakel and Turner suffered minor wounds. The bond that formed during this time had not been broken on their return to postwar San Francisco, and their friendships remained steadfast.

2. Each of the men had amassed a substantial amount of money by midcentury. Fleischakel had left the winery to his son and his other assets to his daughters. Marchand had sold the department store but left a good deal of cash to each of his children. Turner had brought his son into the law firm and left him well provided for. Perlmutter had disinherited his son and sold the taxicab business. Hansen had left his breeding ranch to a daughter who loved horses and a good deal of cash to his son, a documentary filmmaker.

3. Following their arrival at the top of their respective worlds, each had pursued business, charitable, and personal

interests (the latter presumably including their sponsorship of the young lady whose charm they had mutually agreed upon).

4. One investment, the building of a health and tennis spa in Marin County, they had entered into together. Predating the current fad of fitness, it had eventually gone bankrupt.

5. They had all belonged to the Bohemian Club, a near-secret organization of the rich and powerful centered in San Francisco.

6. They had all kept their family life and their lustier interests separate. This equilibrium apparently lasted throughout their lives, since none had divorced.

This, then, was the result of Spencer's morning among the pages of recorded history. It lacked one of those startling revelations which the detective hopes for and the reader comes to expect. Nevertheless, Spencer was satisfied that he had familiarized himself with the dramatis personae. He knew that this case, unlike an hour-long cops and robbers show that must rush headlong to a conclusion in order to maintain the viewer's interest, would be made up of tiny bits and pieces, seemingly ordinary and easily obscured. Eventually, taken together, like the jumbled pieces of a picture puzzle, they would turn into a singular painting of intricate but unified design. It only required painstaking collection of the individual pieces and a master plan for putting each in its proper place.

By the time they were through with the satisfying meal and settled over their coffee, Spencer was confident he had taken a small step toward finding just such a plan. Before he could launch an afternoon of vigorous activity, a telephone call was in order. The waiter brought a phone to the table, plugged the old-fashioned, rotary-dial, black desk model into a jack on the paneled wall behind the booth and left the instrument at Spencer's elbow. He dialed the Pinkerton office.

Preliminaries dispensed with, he heard this report from Louis:

"We took up surveillance Thursday morning. Yesterday. The subject was working in her garden when we arrived at 11:00 A.M. She remained there most of the day. Received no visitors. She went inside at 4:08 P.M., prepared and ate dinner alone. Dressed. Drove to the opera alone at 7:05, meeting no one, but spoke to various members of the audience seated in her vicinity.

All very polite and nothing clandestine. She appeared confused by the events, along with the audience. She left the auditorium with the crowd and drove straight home. On Friday she left the house at 7:00 A.M., drove to the Golden Gate yacht basin, and went sailing with two women friends. Boat is her own, docked there. It's called the *Painted Lady*. She's back at the house now, Delbart is on the scene."

"Thank you, Louis," Spencer said. "Stay with the subject until further notice. And here's something new: you were correct about the murder weapon. It had to be a highly accurate sharpshooter's model. The police are checking out the usual gunsmiths and permit applications, but they won't find anything. This weapon was expressly intended for a single crime and would have been bought anonymously on the black market. Probably only a matter of days or weeks before the crime. See if you can find out anything on the street. A description of the man could be a big help, since he probably used a phony name."

"Got it."

"All right. If there are any unusual developments you know how to reach us. Otherwise I'll check in again tomorrow."

Spencer replaced the receiver thoughtfully. He looked across the tablecloth at Mr. Dihje. You and I would not have read any expression on the impassive face, but Spencer knew his man, and saw an inquisitive interest reflected there.

"She appears to be leading a routine and ordinary life. I suspect the routine is the key."

The waiter returned with the bill and a credit voucher on a plain plastic tray. Spencer signed the slip, took his own copy, and, using his pocket lighter, burned the carbons in the ashtray. It was one of this reasonable man's few eccentricities.

Chapter 7

In which our detective investigates the great yachts of San Francisco.

That afternoon Spencer and Mr. Dihje took a stroll along Fisherman's Wharf. The contrast between what lay on their port and starboard sides was a study in the urban development of a popular city. The wharfside was crowded with fifty-foot skipjacks unloading the morning catch. Weathered fishermen, their skin dry and brown and their eyes permanently squinted from the outdoor life, worked to stow their nets and hose down their decks. Across the narrow, clogged street, packs of polyester tourists, skin pale and eyes shaded with tortoiseshell sun glasses, clustered around T-shirt emporiums, penny souvenir stands, and a wax museum. In between on the sidewalk, vendors sold soft-shell crabs and shrimp at inflated prices.

"Tourists," Spencer grumbled, "have overrun our paradise. Last week I had to wait thirty minutes for a table at the Buena Vista, just for breakfast. They were lined up at the cable turnaround like it was Mr. Toad's Wild Ride. Our city needs to knock off a bit of its charm, or pretty soon it will strangle itself in RV's."

His demeanor brightened as they arrived at the Marina Green harbor. There, just where Louis said it would be, the *Painted Lady* was moored. She was a trim sloop, her sails furled professionally, her decks bright and gleaming. She rode a light swell coming in off the breakwater and strained at her ropes. Spencer could sense how she would sprint gracefully for the ocean at the first opportunity.

"A beautiful lady, just enough worn to be the more attractive. Like her owner. But not what we're here for exactly. The harbormaster is an old friend and will let us peruse the records."

Inside the office, they went through the files, and in twenty minutes Spencer had a certificate in his hands registering another boat to a familiar name.

"Randal Fleischakel. The *Bacchus*. Slip 17. Been here since '75, when his father died, if I recall."

Mr. Dihje closed the file drawer he faced and came to Spencer's side.

"A stinkpot," Spencer said. "A pleasure boat, for those too lazy to seek the real pleasures of the seas. Let's take a look."

Outside once more, they stood this time next to a fifty-foot cruiser, portholes curtained for privacy, decks glassed in against the natural elements of wind and salt spray. She rode low in the water, probably weighted down with custom furnishings. Feeling like pirates, they slipped aboard and toured the deserted yacht.

"A contradiction arises at once," Spencer observed. "See the anchor chain; it is badly curled. The bottom has not been scraped and painted, and needs it. Yet here aboard, the interior is neat and polished, recently cleaned, I would say. Now, why does a man pay more attention to the interior than the seaworthiness of an expensive craft? He is either careless or not. It could be that his wife, domestically oriented, is responsible for the inside while he, sloppy and lazy, takes care of the fittings. That might be building castles in the air, however. No, I think someone has recently seen to a spring cleaning. Someone has gone over the insides thoroughly. In which case, there will be nothing of consequence aboard. We'll return to the office."

But before they could carry out this plan, they were confronted by the sight of a tall, middle-aged man climbing awkwardly aboard. He was clearly not accustomed to the sailor's life, since he wore a three-piece brown suit and wing-tip leather shoes. By the time he had negotiated the gangplank and climbed over the low gate, the men were face-to-face. The newcomer spoke first.

"You Fleischakel?"

"No. Do you have an appointment?"

"An appointment? What are you, his secretary? I want to see Fleischakel."

"That would be difficult. He shuffled off this mortal coil last week."

"He what?"

"He passed away. Deceased. Bought the farm."

"He's dead?"

"Irrevocably."

The man was overcome with suspicion.

"How do I know?" he asked Spencer.

"You don't, apparently. I do. That's why our conversation has turned in this manner."

"Well, I guess it doesn't matter anyway. I can tack this on the door."

"You can tack it on the hatch. There are no doors on a ship. What is it?"

"A dispossess notice." Suddenly the man took a step backward. "You the new owner of this tug?"

"It is not a tug, which is a more specialized ship. I am not. You, I can see now, are a process server. You needn't worry, we have no interest in Fleischakel's financial affairs."

The man relaxed.

"People get pretty upset over this stuff. You never know."

"They execute the bearer of bad news. It is a time-honored tradition. You are safe here—we are interlopers as well."

"You taking the furniture? I don't think that's legal. The contents are part of the notice here."

"No, we were taking stock."

"What stock?"

"Never mind. It's just an expression."

The man, who had become convinced he was not going to be faced with an obstreperous owner, now began to worry that he might be faced with one of San Francisco's unpredictable characters, and backed away.

"I'll just leave this taped to the railing here and go. This is a legal document now. Don't tear it up."

"We are familiar with the workings of the law. You may consider your duty satisfactorily executed."

The man rapidly retreated down the gangplank. A glance at the paper proved it to be authentic. Spencer and Mr. Dihje strolled up the pier again.

That Spencer was not interested in the financial affairs of Randal Fleischakel was not entirely the truth. If Fleischakel had failed to make the payments on a significant piece of property he owned, it meant more than that he was forgetful. The bank would hardly repossess a boat it had no use for until quite a number of monthly payments had gone uncollected, and not without serious attempts at negotiating continued payments with the mortgagee. Clearly, Randal Fleischakel had financial problems, and Spencer found that of interest. In fact, he thought it over for a considerable time as he and Mr. Dihje picked their way through wide-bottomed matrons in pastel sweat suits and took the #30 Stockton, locally known as the Orient Express, for its route through the city's most colorful quarter, downtown.

Chapter 8

A short foray into the unstable world of filmmaking.

Spencer scanned the directory in the lobby of the triangular blue building on the intersection of Broadway and Pacific. Few film tenants remained. The promised renaissance of San Francisco as a major filmmaking center had gone down in the flames of several epic disasters. Nonetheless, Spencer found the suite number he wanted. The elevator wasn't working, so the men walked up three flights of a dingy, dark stairwell to a small corner office bearing the name Hansen Productions.

In the office, a singularly attractive young woman sat glumly at a receptionist's desk. She was weeding through a number of envelopes that had the unmistakable look of requests for funds due. The typewriter did not hum. The phones did not ring. Coils of film sat unattended on a workbench, and more of the same were stacked on a moviola. Dust covered the shelves, and a few charts tacked on various bulletin boards were curled and yellow with age. One glance told Spencer that the first of his two principal theories had been confirmed. Hansen's production company was a bust.

The girl, probably unaccustomed to good news coming through the door, eyed the pair silently.

"Good afternoon, miss. I understand that Robert Hansen has suffered a heart attack. Were you his partner?"

"His partner? I wish. Maybe I could sell some of this crap for a month's wage. I'm the hired help."

"You'll be staying on?"

"No. I'm just trying to organize a few things before I go. Not that anyone's around to care. Hansen Productions has been strictly a one-man outfit for years. Not counting me. I just thought a lawyer or a family member might show up."

"And fulfill Mr. Hansen's commitment re salary owed?"

"Yeah. You wouldn't be his attorney, would you?"

"I'm afraid not. We are, however, attempting to wrap up a few of the details of his former existence. I take it the production company is insolvent?"

At once the woman, clearly interested in her own welfare until now, became reticent.

"I'm not at liberty to discuss the situation."

"Of course, we understand. My name is Spencer Holmes, and this is Sowhat Dihje. We are doing an article on the life and work of Mr. Hansen for *Films and Filmmaking*.

"You're journalists?"

"That's correct. We would like to put together a piece on Hansen's documentaries."

The shot in the dark was not altogether wide, if naive.

"Documentaries? Say, you guys go back a while, don't you? He hasn't made a documentary since I've been here, which is two years now. But I guess you guys aren't going to review his recent work, are you?"

"Actually, I understand he was in the middle of a project the week he died. That would make an excellent touch. We can call it 'The Unfinished Film.' "

"What magazine did you say you were from?"

"Films and Filmmaking? It's very prestigious. Only features auteurs."

"Then you aren't interested in his uncompleted oeuvre. For the last couple of years he's been shooting Tits and Clits."

"I beg your pardon?"

"You know, skin flicks. Porno."

Understanding dawned.

"I see. If I'm not mistaken, that is an almost certainly profitable venture . . . though not for actors and actresses." He hoped this subtle hint might lodge in the woman's subconscious, at the very least. "I cannot help but notice your suite is less than luxuriously furnished. I regret returning to a subject of privacy." He appended this last so as not to seem rude. The girl forgot her reticence, however.

"It wasn't profitable here. He didn't have the capital to invest. You seen the competition lately?"

The girl went right on, and Spencer was fortunately not pressed to commit himself.

"Full color, exotic sets and props. First-class lighting and camera work. Two-inch video master. They come in at anywhere between $250,000 and $750,000. Bobby was still making 16mm black-and-white stag films for Elks smokers."

"Behind the times, was he?"

"Oh, he was an all-right guy, don't get me wrong. But he never made a splash in the documentary field, and after a few decades of trying he'd run through his daddy's money. He was still trying to recoup when he died."

"He was working on a feature then?"

"Well, he was starting to. Last weekend he had me rent him some equipment. Good stuff, too. I had to do some swift talking, I can tell you, to get it all on credit. The bills are here somewhere, I'm sure. Now what am I going to do?"

"Our readers are particularly interested in the technical aspects of filmmaking . . . ?"

"He did it all. Different positions, oral sex, girls with girls, leather, harnesses—"

"No, no, no. I mean the equipment. The filmmaking equipment. What, for example, was he renting last weekend?"

"Last weekend I got him a Steadicam. He was going to try to do something special."

"Were you with him all the time?"

"No. I didn't help him with any of the production work. I ran the office, did his correspondence. He free-lanced a sound man usually, and rented a house or a motel room."

"Where was he last weekend?"

"I don't know. He made the arrangements himself."

"And the equipment was back here Monday morning?"

"He took it in himself. He said he'd gotten what he wanted and the actors weren't available again until next weekend. He generally used college girls. They don't like to miss their classes."

Spencer had not only gotten the information he had come for, he had gotten a good deal more. Apparently his understanding of college coeds needed some expansion. That was an investigation which would have to wait. He and Mr. Dihje edged for the door.

"Thank you very much, miss. You have been most helpful."

"You're not going to write about the hard-core stuff, are you?

He had a lot of classy friends. I don't think his latest projects were common knowledge."

"Oh, no. We'll just say he was hard at work on a film of . . . modern relationships, when he passed away."

"Good. He'd like that, I'm sure."

"Fine. Well then, good afternoon. And thanks again."

On the way home, the detective pondered two newly discovered facts from the life of Robert Hansen. He had run through his inheritance, and he had recently rented a unique piece of cineaste equipment. Mr. Dihje, disappointed that a viewing of the subject's most recent work had not been necessary, gazed upon each female figure carrying schoolbooks with new appreciation.

Chapter 9

Interlude.

As inappropriate to a satisfactorily rising line of dramatic action as it might be, that evening the detective and his assistant stayed home.

After dinner they retired to the library, where they sat before a fire, reading. As the embers died down, however, Spencer looked up from his book and stared into the fireplace. After a few moments of quiet contemplation, he opened the conversation.

"In my grandfather's time," Spencer said to Mr. Dihje, in his habit of launching into a subject without preliminaries, "the world was a sane and organized place."

"For the Englishman," Mr. Dihje interjected.

"Well, yes. For the Englishman. He was at the calm center of the greatest empire in history. There was a standard of justice, against which behavior was judged. There was aberrant behavior, crimes against society and individuals. But they were the exception to the rule of order. Grandfather Sherlock abhorred crime, because he abhorred injustice. Any attack on the social contract which human beings held with each other was a personal insult to him. Did you know that he was known as the Hound of Justice, among other epithets which attached to him over the years? Quite poetic, I think." And Spencer thought about it for a moment.

"Grandfather's quest was a clear one," Spencer eventually went on. "He was a surgeon of society, cutting out the malignant tumors where he found them."

"A best and wisest man," Mr. Dihje nodded.

"Exactly. You will recall, however, that he didn't succeed."

Mr. Dihje, who had been listening thoughtfully while following Spencer's gaze into the fireplace, turned to Spencer, puzzled.

"Oh, yes," Spencer went on. "He successfully concluded a great number of cases in his long life."

"Except one."

"Except one," Spencer chuckled. "And we have Grandmother to thank for that. But, in the end, his mission, if we can assume he had one, didn't succeed. He could not stem the rising tide of violence. You will recall his last case, for example. When he successfully exposed and captured the German spy Von Bork. Even then he knew in his heart, as he sat on his beloved English Downs and looked into the future, that he could not stop what he called that evil wind rising from the East."

"Eventually World Wars One and Two each successfully concluded, I think," Mr. Dihje volunteered.

"They were. But at what a cost. We are now armed to the teeth with weapons, any one of which is a thousand times greater than the bomb which shocked the world. There are over a hundred armed conflicts proceeding viciously somewhere in the world right now. And while society fights everywhere against totalitarianism, there is an even worse cancer multiplying in what passes for civilized society."

Mr. Dihje leaned in curiously, and Spencer Holmes lowered his voice for emphasis.

"Moral degeneration. What do you think Grandfather would say about an entire company which sells a product it knows to be defective, but hides the truth in order to pursue its profits? What would he say about a conglomeration that requires the destruction of the rain forests just to present its products in enticing packages? What would he say about government officials selling their influence? Not one bad apple, but hundreds in a single administration? He was not unaccustomed to murder, but the murder of thousands of innocent citizens every year? And society too busy to create adequate programs to stop this madness? Would he believe it if I could tell him that we can no longer safely swim in our own rivers? That hundreds of people die every year from the very air they breathe? That we are attempting to cure any number of body cancers, but unable, because of our commitment to increasing profits at any cost, to stem the tide of pollution that is the greatest cause of these cancers? What would he say, my friend?"

Mr. Dihje was silent.

"And if our whole society is as selfish and uncaring as all that, how can we expect the disenfranchised not to rise up and demand their share, whether by mugging an old lady in the street, robbing a bank, or engaging in worldwide terrorism against the haves? I think Grandfather knew there would be no stopping Moriarty or his kind, for they would take new names and new identities in future ages. And I think he would not be surprised, were he alive today, to find that the Moriartys of the world have proliferated."

"We must stop them."

"We cannot stop them. Because a just man must operate by the rules of decency and common sense, but an unjust man, why, he can ignore rules, and thus will operate always at a greater advantage."

Spencer fought off an enveloping feeling of depression, and leaned back in his chair. After a long pause, Mr. Dihje spoke up.

"Why we be detectives then?" he asked. "Why fight injustice?"

"Why, indeed, Mr. Dihje. For myself, I feel an obligation to carry on Grandfather's noble work. He and my father left me enough money to live comfortably. That is my greatest freedom. How many people are completely free, really free, to choose how they will spend their life? At the same time, it is my greatest obligation. To choose wisely. Life itself is our greatest gift. We all have to answer for it. We have to look life straight in the eye. Without blinking. Look neither left nor right. Not be seduced by avarice into taking a wrong turn. So many of our most privileged citizens are no longer honest men. In many ways, our Constitution protects them too well, for our Constitution was framed by men who assumed honesty as a given. Now we have to stop this mad rush toward selfishness. As Tolstoy said, if evil men can get together to accomplish what they want, why can't good men get together to accomplish what they want? In any case, to give up the fight, no matter how hopeless-seeming, is to give up our humanity. And to give up our humanity is to deny our very existence."

Spencer got up and walked softly to the window, where he stood, staring out.

Mr. Dihje, knowing that the next day would be at least as hectic as the last, rose, brushed a few stray embers back into the fireplace, put out all but one light, and went across the hall to his own room, where he quickly fell into a restless slumber. Spencer stayed at the window gazing out over the city from the dimly lit room, where the single lamp threw his tall, wiry silhouette onto the wall. It wavered there, like a contemporary Don Quixote, for several mute minutes. Then he retired for the night.

Elsewhere, Louis took his assigned turn sleeping in the Buick parked beneath the redwood house on the hill, where no one stirred.

Harrington and his daughter played tennis in the cool night air under expensive silicon lighting and the watchful eye of Delbart of the Pinkertons.

In short, nothing happened.

Chapter 10

In which the detective and his companion close in on a geographical area of mounting importance to their investigation.

On Saturday morning, when the bay was once again dotted with sailboats leaning into the wind and the wharf was choked with visitors, Spencer and Mr. Dihje dressed in their tennis whites, tested the strings of their favorite rackets, and piloted their stately automobile across the Golden Gate Bridge.

There is no sense in disguising the fact that Spencer was combining business with pleasure. Troubled in recent weeks with a waffling backhand, he was determined to correct it. And the concerns of recent investigations had limited his ordinary schedule of exercise. As for Mr. Dihje, he was delighted for the opportunity to burn calories, and was already calculating the amount he could justifiably replace. Their particular destination, however, was provoked by Louis, who had shadowed his subject, and called in her current whereabouts to Spencer. This morning Sarah Bernstein was playing tennis at the North Bay Tennis Club. Spencer explained their destination to Mr. Dihje.

"You recall that when we visited her last Wednesday, she had just come in from riding. Thursday night she attended the opera. Friday she went sailing. We don't need to track her movements on Monday and Tuesday to see that she is *still following the routine of her former life.* Still pursuing the interests bequeathed to her by her benefactors, as she illustrated to us in her description of her life with them. She is, in fact, still on the same schedule. Wednesday riding, Thursday opera, Friday sailing."

"Today Saturday."

"Yes. And here she is, playing tennis, which she probably does fairly regularly, or she wouldn't have had three tennis rackets in her study. Did you see them there in the corner? And what business did the men engage in together? A tennis club. Interesting, eh? Let us assume her Saturdays are for tennis. When did this come about? And why?"

This morning when they arrived she was having a lesson with the local pro, a handsome young man half her age with unruly straw hair and flashing blue eyes. Spencer and Mr. Dihje slowed their car to a stop outside the fence, where they watched Sarah and the young pro. Spencer was impressed with her manner of attacking the ball before it attacked her. She did not suffer from the customary female fear of moving projectiles. She didn't push at it, but had a smooth, powerful stroke. She ran to meet it gracefully. While Spencer calculated her age to be forty-one, she had the game of a twenty-five-year-old. Right now she was being coached to serve a wickedly spinning ball to the inside corner of the service box. Spencer made a mental note to pull his backhand.

He left the car and headed up a wide brick staircase lined with ivy, where he was approached by a middle-aged woman wearing a blue vest with a club insignia on the breast. Mr. Dihje wheeled the car around and headed for a parking spot in the shade of a large oak tree.

The woman extended a jeweled hand to Spencer.

"Mr. Holmes? I'm Candace Lawrence, membership secretary. Mr. Harrington said you would be paying us a visit. We're delighted to have you as our guest today."

"Thank you, Miss Lawrence. Your club is beautiful."

"We have a very exclusive membership, and very particular. A bit conservative, perhaps, but very friendly. I can introduce you to some excellent players for both singles and doubles, if you'd care to arrange a game. The swimming pool is always available and the kitchen will open at noon and remain open the rest of the day. Just sign your name to bar and restaurant checks, please. You're Mr. Harrington's guest. The pro shop is off the main patio, in there."

Miss Lawrence extended a tan arm and pointed across the terrace as she accompanied Spencer up the broad steps.

"Thank you. May I ask how long you've been with the club?"

"Nineteen years, since it was formed. Since then we've doubled the number of courts and added a great number of facilities. Many of our families have been with us from the beginning."

"It was my understanding that the club was originally open to the public."

"I'm afraid I don't know about that, but the main buildings and court were here when we moved in."

"Who was occupying them then?"

"They were deserted. Apparently another organization of some sort had sold the property."

"I wonder why."

"Financial difficulties was the rumor at the time, I understand. I really don't know much about that, but you see the man sitting at the end of the patio by the stairs? In the red warm-up suit?"

"Yes."

"He is the club's president, Henry Sappington. He was one of the original members and is quite familiar with the details of the club's history. I'll introduce you."

"That would be excellent, thank you."

Sappington seemed to be holding court with a handful of young male and female club attendants when Spencer arrived. They disappeared quickly, using his arrival, Spencer suspected, as an excuse. Before long the two men were seated facing each other. Sappington was a large, florid man, made larger by the sun's reflection on the broad satin material wrapped around his body and a towel draped around his neck. The man's voice fairly boomed, but by sitting close to him and lowering his own, Spencer managed to keep the conversation down to the immediate circle of tables which, thanks to the pre-noon hour, were empty. He introduced himself as a good friend of Wilkesford Harrington.

"The Harringtons are one of our oldest families," the man said in a low roar. "His daughter has been taking lessons here for years. I was sorry to hear about the death of her young man. And under such circumstances too."

"You've heard about it, then?"

"Oh, yes. The grisly details weren't in the papers; I suppose Harrington saw to that. But a private country club is a hotbed of gossip, as I guess you know. Why, half the members were there. The Harringtons are very popular, I can tell you."

"I understand you are one of the founders."

"That's right. I was on the financial committee when we founded this place. The courts in the area were getting crowded with the Marin element, if you know what I mean. A number of older families decided a private club would be more to their liking."

"Before that, this was a public health club, I believe."

"Yes. I don't think we called them health clubs in those days. It was the . . ."

"Marin Tennis Club."

"That's right. We changed the name."

"Why was it for sale?"

"Bankrupt! The developer—a local tennis pro—got in over his head. He bought the land and built the facilities, ran it for less than a year. He was underfinanced. He had some silent partners who were supposed to underwrite the project. According to him, they backed out and left him without adequate financing. Finally he was forced to declare bankruptcy and sell the property. We heard about it from someone, I don't remember who, and put a bid together. Exclusivity, that was the key. We were completely subscribed within three months. Memberships are rarely available; there's a waiting list even if you're approved by the committee. Any friend of Harrington's, of course . . ."

The man left the invitation dangling. Spencer assured him he found the facilities first class.

"We don't let anything go, I can tell you. Today, you can't go anywhere that isn't full of undesirable elements. I can see you're a man of breeding and background. You're anxious to associate with your own ki—"

The man cut himself off in midsentence and stared over Spencer's shoulder, where Mr. Dihje stood quietly loosening up his racket arm. Spencer went on smoothly.

"This is my doubles partner, Mr. Dihje. Mr. Dihje, Mr. Sappington.

Mr. Sappington's demeanor had been transformed by the arrival of Mr. Dihje, whose brown face matched the shade of tan being desperately cultivated by a number of women lounging by the pool.

Mr. Dihje extended his hand. Sappington took it reluctantly. Mr. Dihje also nodded and smiled. Mr. Sappington nodded. Spencer continued.

"You were saying, Mr. Sappington?"

"What were we talking about? I'm afraid I've forgotten."

"It doesn't matter. Well, we've got a court scheduled for eleven o'clock; I think we'll visit the pro shop and purchase some new balls. It was a pleasure to meet you, Mr. Sappington."

"Give my regards to Mr. Harrington."

"I will."

The tennis players walked to the clubhouse. The fortunate coincidence sometimes awarded to the diligent detective then arose. In the clubhouse, Sarah Bernstein had just arrived with her teacher.

Chapter 11

A second encounter with the principal asset of the Weekday Club.

"Miss Bernstein! How delightful to see you." Spencer quickly extended his hand.

"Why, Mr . . . ?"

"Spencer. Spencer Holmes. And you recall my associate, Mr. Sowhat Dihje." The man bowed deeply.

"Yes, of course." Miss Bernstein hesitated, then glanced uncomfortably from the tennis pro to a young woman behind the counter.

"We met at the opera. I'm Wilkesford Harrington's friend."

The woman immediately relaxed. She understood at once that Spencer had no intention of exposing the unusual circumstances of her past.

"I couldn't help admiring your service form just now. You play very well."

"Thank you. I didn't know you were a member here."

"Just a guest for the day. Perhaps we could have a game or two."

"Perhaps we could."

"Good. This afternoon then? Shall we say one o'clock? Just the two of us." Spencer impressed this last remark on the woman with a quiet smile and a penetrating glance.

"All right. I'll look for you. Now, if you'll excuse me, I have a lunch date."

She left the room. Spencer hoped he hadn't scared her. He knew that his presence alone, especially to those who knew his profession, could be unsettling. He looked forward to their match, as a means of improving his game and obtaining information he was convinced she had withheld at their first meeting.

Now he found her teacher hovering over him. The young man was friendly.

"I'm Mark Shawn. One of the teaching pros here. You'll have a tough game. Miss Bernstein is an excellent player. I don't think I've seen you here before."

"We're guests. Of Wilkesford Harrington."

"Oh, yes."

If Spencer had sensed in the man a protective interest in his pupil, he now became aware of another shift in atmosphere. The young man seemed nervous, shifting back and forth from one foot to the other.

"How long have you been working with her?"

"Just this summer. I go to Berkeley; I'm on the team there. My coach got me this job for the summer."

"How do you like it?"

"I like it awfully well. Especially when I can work with a really good player like Miss Bernstein."

"Then there are the hackers."

The young man smiled.

"I guess you've been around the game before. Sure, a pro has to work with a lot of different people. It can be pretty frustrating. You want to tell them to forget it, they're never going to find the ball. But everyone, almost everyone, is very nice. And the staff tournament is brutal; you'd be amazed. I've been able to improve my own game here, too, I think."

Spencer had wandered over to a wall covered with plaques and photographs, and a glass case containing trophies. By way of explanation, the pro spoke behind him.

"The Northern California AAU finals are held here. Plus amateur tournaments."

"Does Sarah Bernstein play in the club tournaments?"

"I don't really know. I would assume so. If you'll excuse me, I have an eleven o'clock waiting for me." He scooped up a basketful of balls and headed down the steps outside.

Spencer eyed the wall. Mr. Dihje came to his side. Spencer lowered his voice.

"Whether young Mark Shawn knows it or not, Sarah Bernstein has been playing tournaments here for a long time. Mixed doubles. Pro-member division. Won it in 1965 and '66. She and her partner have their names inscribed right here."

Mr. Dihje stepped up to get a closer look. Over Spencer's extended finger he read "Sarah Bernstein, Matthew Adler." Next to the inscription, there was a photograph of the two, with their arms around a trophy and each other.

Chapter 12

Game, set, with match delayed.

On the court that afternoon Spencer met his match.

Winning the toss, she elected to serve first. Envisioning the inside spin he had witnessed her practice earlier, he was prepared to return with a backhand when she ripped the ball past his forehand. He returned the ad-court serve, traded ground strokes for several volleys, and then rushed the net, feeling her first serve had sufficiently embarrassed him to allow for aggressive play without appearing overly chauvinistic. She hit a forehand down the line that passed him neatly.

"Thirty–love," Mr. Dihje announced implacably from his seat in the shade.

Her next serve was long. Unhappily for Spencer's calculations, her second serve was as thundering as her first, and it caught him flat-footed.

"Forty–love."

Spencer saved his pride with a long, safe series of ground strokes which kept his opponent at the baseline. He played defensively—a tactic he was afraid could result in his ultimate defeat—until he caught the tape by mistake. The ball dribbled over and even Stan Smith couldn't have reached it.

"Forty–five." Did Spencer detect a subtle hint of disappointment in his friend's voice?

The first game ended when Spencer watched the spinning serve to his backhand kick out of reach. It was the serve he had reminded himself to watch out for. He decided against trying to outguess his opponent and made a note to adjust his position accordingly. As they changed sides, Spencer opened the conversation.

"I'm afraid I'm not giving you much of a game."

"You're still warming up. Is this really a coincidence, Mr. Holmes?"

"Not exactly. I knew you played here on weekends."

"Then you're still investigating. You suspect me."

"Oh, no. The man I'm looking for is . . . a man. I had him in my arms briefly. He was disguised, but very strong."

"I'm very strong."

"I can see that. You have other, uh, attributes that were not present, if I may be so bold."

The woman smiled.

"I'm not a suspect, then?"

"I'm afraid I cannot confirm that either just yet. The case has become increasingly complex. Conspiracy is almost certainly involved. Please do not take this as an insult: right now, we suspect everyone and no one, as the old saying goes.

He took his place on the court and toed the line.

He just managed to hold serve with a combination of luck, cautious play, and exhausting coverage of the court, which, due to the height advantage he enjoyed over his opponent, was his only hole card. The game went to deuce. He rushed the net behind his first serve unexpectedly, then backpedaled just in time to hit an overhead smash. At ad-in he almost got trapped on the wrong side of the court, but reached the ball just in time to flip it back halfheartedly. She didn't expect it to go over.

"One game all." Mr. Dihje settled back to witness a long set.

In the third game, Spencer forced himself to react quickly, and managed to return all of her serves. Nevertheless, a sudden affinity for the forecourt on her part, combined with an approach shot which put Spencer in precisely the worst spot to return the ball, gave her a two-to-one advantage. They changed sides again.

"You were, however, at the opera last Thursday night when the son of Mr. Thursday was murdered."

"I go to the opera every Thursday; I have a subscription."

"You don't seem to be overly concerned."

"I didn't know Carl's children. I read about it in the paper. They said it was an accident. Do all detectives assume the worst?"

"That isn't the worst. The eldest son of each of your lovers has been killed recently." Spencer faced her directly when he said this. She was either an extraordinary actress, or honestly startled. After a long moment, and her request that he repeat the information, she recovered her composure.

"And you think I have something to do with this."

"Of course you have *something* to do with it. Those five men had you in common. Your daughter's happiness was recently curtailed with the murder of her fiancé, and the death of their five sons rapidly followed. Good heavens, you are practically in the center of the thing."

"I can't imagine why. My life was with their fathers, and that ended a long time ago."

"And you have never introduced yourself to the girl Felicity?"

"Never. She can petition the court for her files, discover my identity, and seek me out if she wants to. I have left that up to her. I think that's the right thing to do, don't you?"

"It is a complex situation. I don't envy your position. I suppose if she were to track you down, she'd ask about her father."

"Yes. I suppose she would."

Spencer felt sorry for this woman whose youth had been misspent. Now she was paying the price.

"You kept track of her, however?"

"All right. I wasn't telling you the whole truth the last time we met. You caught me by surprise and I wasn't sure how much I wanted to say. I did know who adopted her. I don't know the Harringtons personally and have made it my business to avoid them. They are not aware that I'm her natural mother. They've done a wonderful job of raising my baby. I see her here at the club sometimes; it is very gratifying. I knew she was getting married; their family is often in the social columns. And I heard about the murder. Then you showed up."

"And you never introduced yourself to her."

"I wanted to many times. But I didn't think that was my right. I didn't even know if the Harringtons had told her she was adopted, though later I found out that they had. I thought about it a great deal, especially after my friends were gone. Finally I decided it would be rude to pop up and announce myself. Threatening to her adoptive parents in a way, and emotionally jarring to a young girl. I decided it should be her decision. If she wants to meet her natural mother, she only has to ask the court for the papers. Perhaps someday she will."

It was clear to Spencer that Sarah hoped for that day.

She walked onto the court.

Apparently sensitive subjects had no effect upon her game. She returned his best serves effortlessly and ran down every ball with ease. This broke Spencer's serve and put him behind three games to one. He resolved to break back immediately, so as to avoid giving her the advantage of too much momentum.

With her first service he went on the attack. She played to his forehand and he returned down the line, catching her attempting to rush the net. Then he rushed the net himself and achieved a crosscourt backhand. When she double-faulted for the first time he found himself in control of the game, at which point he grew overconfident and she saved three game points, bringing the score to deuce.

With her next serve he anticipated an approach and aimed for the far corner. He was rewarded. His next return went flat into her and she blocked it for a brilliant drop shot. Deuce again. She served and they traded ground strokes half a dozen times. Too late, he realized she was working him into the sidelines. She put her next forehand out of his reach without effort.

"Ad in."

"Thank you, Mr. Dihje. I am aware of the score," Spencer called out. Mr. Dihje looked unconcernedly at Miss Bernstein.

Sarah's first serve caught the tape.

"Let," the three said at once, raising the level of intensity measurably.

Her second serve shot to his backhand. He lifted it deep to her forehand. She returned and approached the net. He found the ball in the air by his right shoulder and the woman waiting for him. Resisting the instinct to smash it cleanly, he blocked it to her forehand, and she volleyed to the opposite court for the game.

"You mustn't be timid, Mr. Holmes. Just because I'm a woman."

"No. I see that now."

They changed sides in silence.

In the sixth game, Spencer took shameless advantage of his physical superiority, running the woman back and forth until she drove the ball an inch too deep or too wide. Then he

changed tactics and rushed the net for several points. He eked
out a two-point win.

"Four–two." There was a hint of admiration in Mr. Dihje's
voice.

She chose to attack his backhand consistently with the serve
she had spent a part of the morning perfecting. It paid off. His
backhand, inconsistent at best, deserted him under pressure
and she held serve easily.

With five games to his two, she loosened up, and opened the
conversation on the changeover.

"I didn't know any of the victims. What could this possibly
have to do with me?"

"Your benefactors had provided for your daughter with a
trust fund that came to a substantial sum of money. The trust,
however, dictated that in order to collect, she was to be married
no later than her twenty-first birthday. When her fiancé was
killed, the money fell to their oldest sons. The sequence of
murders puts it out of their hands, but the connection exists
nevertheless."

"The men knew each other long before they met me. They
were in the army together and in business together."

"That is not quite true. They were in the army together and
remained friends, but were only in business together on one
occasion, and that after they had . . . sponsored . . . you.
The original Marin Tennis Club, which included the courts we
stand on now."

"What?" Sarah looked startled.

Spencer had hit on something that had shaken her. He explained.

"They were the investment team behind the original Marin
Tennis Club. It was unsuccessful and they took a loss, which
I'm sure they could well afford. It was then that it went private
and cooperative, and the North Bay Club took over the property."

"And Matthew Adler went bankrupt."

"The Adler who was your tennis partner?"

Sarah Bernstein sat down. She adjusted her headband.

"Yes. Matt was a local pro and my teacher. We played
doubles together quite often. It was he who built this place. Put
his life savings into it. When it went bankrupt, he had his first

heart attack and had to stop playing. Two years later he was dead. He was only forty-one." Sarah looked off over the courts. "I had no idea they were his investors."

"Did Adler leave any relatives?"

"He was never married. There was a sister, as I recall, from Nevada." She stood up and walked to her position.

Spencer unmercifully pressed the advantage of serving, flinging caution to the wind—the last refuge of the underdog—and coming in behind almost every serve. She was distracted—either by their conversation or his tactics—and Spencer held serve.

She pulled herself together in the very next game. Her first serve caught the outside edge of the line for an ace. Spencer drifted to the ad court. He returned her next serve, then saved a potential volley by lobbing the ball just over her head.

"Five all."

The next serve went wide. He returned her second serve, advanced to the net, and saved a passing shot by diving for the ball. He wondered if his ignominious drop to the ground was worth a point.

"Five–thirty."

Sarah Bernstein served to his backhand, raced to the net, and casually blocked his return.

"Thirty all."

She repeated the maneuver. This time he lobbed her. She backpedaled and smashed an overhead out of his reach.

"Set point."

Spencer contented himself with glowering at Mr. Dihje.

She put a serve to his backhand, but he had expected that she would attempt to put the game away with her most recent lesson. For three exchanges he kept her behind the baseline. Then he miscalculated and a forehand fell short. She approached the net quickly, scooping up the ball and laying it into the far corner. Calculating he could neither pass nor lob her, he drove the ball as hard as he could straight toward her. It was an awkward return, blocked directly in front of her, and Spencer had just time to reach the ball and send it back over the net. She walked to it, and with a graceful backhand loaded with top spin, put it back exactly where he had been. He watched it bounce in the corner, then turned to his opponent.

"Nicely played. You have my utmost admiration. I have seldom seen a finer woman athlete. We must do this again."

"Are you trying to hustle me, Mr. Holmes?"

"No, ma'am. Not at all. I was wondering, however, the same thing."

The two players, soaked with sweat, and breathing heavily, smiled at each other. Neither was quite clear whether they were antagonists off the court or not.

"Miss Bernstein, I—"

"Sarah."

"Sarah. I would like you to know that my only interest is to see that justice is done in the matter of the young man's murder. I'm sorry if my investigations bisect your personal life."

"I appreciate that, Mr. Holmes."

"Spencer."

"Spencer. I am naturally anxious that no harm should come to Felicity, whatever this is all about. And of course, that her fiancé's murderer be apprehended. I would like to help you all I can."

"And yet the first time we met, you didn't admit to any knowledge of your daughter."

"The first time we met I had no real idea who you were. Since then I've learned a bit more about you. It seems you are quite famous in San Francisco circles." She smiled at him, and he knew that smile had in its day stopped the hearts of at least five men.

"I am flattered. I think. I hope my bona fides has convinced you to tell me everything you know."

"And I have. Everything I can."

Sarah Bernstein walked out the gate and climbed the stairs to the terrace. Spencer watched her disappear into the dressing rooms. He thought of the photograph of the triumphant doubles team, taken more than a decade ago.

Mr. Dihje trotted onto the court. For the next hour, Spencer made him pay for what he perceived as a wanton disregard for loyalty to his employer.

On their way home, Mr. Dihje applied bandages to the blisters on his heels while Spencer drove. Outside of whistling the soprano aria from *Carmen,* Spencer's sole attempt at conversation was an oblique one.

"Did you get a good look at the tennis pro in the pro shop?"
he queried. "Mark Shawn. I could swear we've seen him somewhere before. . . . I have it—he was at the wedding. I saw him
among the guests that afternoon. A friend of the family, I wonder? Curious. We must find out more about him."

Chapter 13

Our detective begins to see the forest through the family trees.

Early the next morning Spencer telephoned the Pinkerton office to receive their daily report. Louis had found a black-market gun salesman who had sold an expensive sharpshooter's rifle, unregistered and without a permit, two weeks before. Because the man refused to meet them during the day, Spencer made arrangements to pick up Louis at Enrico's at ten o'clock that evening. Then he drove to Berkeley.

The University of California campus is not like other college campuses across the United States. Very little adherence to preppy style is in evidence. Oh, there are lettermen cardigans and plaid skirts in abundance. But these are mixed with boys and girls in torn denims and faded sweatshirts carrying backpacks, who in turn blend in among pipe-smoking, bearded youths toting worn briefcases, who disappear among the shaved-head-wrapped-in-bedsheet contingent, who share the sidewalk with young adults from the pages of *Vogue* and *Gentleman's Quarterly.* Two characters like Spencer Holmes, outfitted by Banana Republic, and Sowhat Dihje, in a brocade mandarin jacket and burlap peasant slacks, caused no undue stir on the grounds. They blended in easily, and no one glanced at them twice.

They edged past a dozen pale men and women who were chained to bicycle racks spread across the library steps. They avoided a C.I.A. recruiting table and detainment by a young man bearing a petition to end world hunger. They strolled by a sorority football game conducted in a pit of mud and loudly encouraged by a contingent of oafish young men drinking beer. They climbed a narrow street into the hills, until they finally reached their destination.

The man who opened the door of the small ivy-shrouded

house could only have been a professor of medieval languages. Thick glasses gave him a bemused expression. Shaggy gray hair fell around his ears. The shoulders of a rumpled corduroy jacket were flaked with dandruff. A raven perched upon his shoulder would not have surprised Spencer. In any case, a parrot stood on the branch of a potted tree in the hallway.

"Yes?"

"Professor Shawn? My name is Spencer Holmes. This is Mr. Sowhat Dihje. We have an appointment for two o'clock. I hope we're not unreasonably early."

"Yes, yes. Come in. I'm just at the end of a tutorial. Why don't you make yourself comfortable here."

He led them into a living room, chiefly furnished with books. A garden, overgrown to the point of barring penetrators, was in view beyond the windows. Spencer and Mr. Dihje sat in faded armchairs and eavesdropped on a timid undergraduate. Voices floated in from the next room.

". . . and Hamlet's stepfather is covertly homosexual. He is at once aroused and frightened by Hamlet, who threatens his marriage of convenience with Gertrude. Hamlet's love for his mother is unnatural, and he is anxious to take his deceased father's place. Of course he is tortured by these oedipal feelings, yet welcomes the chance to do away with anyone who might stand between him and his mother."

"Good heavens, boy, who's been filling your head with such garbage!"

"Well, sir, Professor Freulich points out—"

"Freulich! Freulich is a Freudian! Even Freud wasn't a Freudian by the time he died! Hamlet's father was murdered. His throne was usurped. He encourages his son to seek revenge. But Hamlet's a timid man. He doesn't know what to do. He can't make up his mind, that's all. He's a man who can't make up his mind!"

"But when he kills Laertes, his latent jealousy toward—"

"Blood and thunder, boy, blood and thunder! How do you think Shakespeare kept the crowd's attention? The pit was a surly mob, drifting around, talking back to the actors, greeting each other. He had to entertain them. Don't you go to the movies?"

"Yes, sir."

"And when does the audience pay attention? During the fighting, that's when. It was no different in Shakespeare's time. A few good duels, that's what was needed. Action, adventure . . ."

The sounds emanating from the parlor indicated that Professor Shawn was illustrating his thesis. Thrusts, parries, and lunges echoed throughout the small house. Shortly the door swung open, and a ginger-haired young man backed out of the room. The professor, flailing an umbrella, backed the boy through the room into the hall. The boy, using his books as a shield, was beating a hasty retreat.

"Yes, Professor Shawn. I see. I'll take a closer look at the text from that point of view. Same time next week, then? Good-bye, sir."

Clutching the doorknob with his free hand, the young man edged out, pulling it shut behind him with a loud bang. At once the tousled professor ceased the attack, dropped the umbrella into a hollow elephant's foot that stood near the door, and came back into the living room, blithely unaware that he had created a scene. He sat down on a couch opposite his visitors.

"There is altogether too much *thinking* in the field of classical drama today. Timing, pacing, get your laughs. That is what the theatre is about. That is what it has always been about. Mesmerizing the audience. Sets, pageantry, good-looking women. Don't you agree?"

"My own tastes do run to the *Sturm und Drang* on the stage, I must confess," Spencer said.

"None of this namby-pamby direction, everybody walking around thinking about their mothers. Action and reaction, that's just what we need. Now, what can I do for you?"

"It's about your son, Mark."

"Mark? What's he done?"

A parent, Spencer reflected, is never far from anxiety where his children are concerned. Spencer rushed to mollify him, in the hope that he had not begun the interview on the wrong foot.

"Nothing, nothing whatsoever. I saw him only yesterday on the courts. At the top of his form he was, I assure you. Quite the opposite, we are considering him for a scholarship, and we like to interview the parents as part of the application process. Education is a family matter, we believe."

"I didn't know he'd applied for a scholarship."

"He hasn't. We are an unusual organization, in that respect. We do not wait for talent to come to us, we seek it out. He is being considered for this year's Mycroft scholarship."

"I don't believe I've ever heard of that one."

"Well, we like to keep a low profile. It's for graduate study. We seek a combination of athletic prowess and academic achievement. We prefer to keep things confidential, by the way, so as not to disappoint anyone. There are a number of other candidates being considered."

"I understand. How can I help?"

"If you could simply fill in a bit of his background, it would be of great use to us."

"That's a bit vague; I'm not precisely sure what you want."

"Oh, anything that you think would resound to his credit. Anything at all."

"You must have his grades, I assume, and you've witnessed his athletic abilities . . ."

"Yes. What about his extracurricular activities? When did he start teaching at the country club?"

"Early this summer. His coach got him the job. Last summer he was a counselor at a tennis camp."

"How long has he been playing tennis?"

"Almost all his life. Lessons were free at the local YMCA when he was a child. My wife took him once a week, and he took to it like a duck to water."

"Neither of you played?"

"Oh, no."

"He gets his academic prowess from you, undoubtedly."

"We've encouraged him to study hard, of course. There is no substitute for a solid grounding in the classics. Lately he has demonstrated an affinity for the computer, I'm sorry to say. Still, I suppose it does have its uses."

"Has he always had excellent grades?"

"Well, I don't know what your qualifications are. His grade point has always wavered between B-plus and A-minus."

"Was he a boy scout?"

"I'm afraid not."

Spencer gradually drew the professor out on the subject of his son. It was not easy. A certain academic aloofness characterized his qualified judgments, though there was no lack of love for his offspring. He simply did not see his boy through the rose-colored glasses most progenitors do. At the end of an hour, Spencer's powers of improvisation were nearly exhausted. The professor was still game, but clearly wondering about the parameters of the scholarship.

Spencer gave up. There was nothing more to uncover. The trip, prompted by his own desire to leave no stone unturned, had been a washout.

"You've been a great help," Spencer lied. "I'm certain the boy stands an excellent chance for the scholarship. We won't take up any more of your time."

They all stood up. At the door, Spencer thanked him again.

"The interview with the family is always most rewarding. There's nothing like strong genes. You can be most proud."

"Thank you. I'm afraid, of course, that I cannot take credit for his genes."

"I don't think I quite catch your drift?"

"Oh, of course. There's no reason you would have known. We adopted Mark at birth."

Spencer, at long last, was thunderstruck.

Chapter 14

Spencer and Mr. Dihje make one final inquiry.

Spencer and Mr. Dihje drove back across the Bay Bridge in silence. Mr. Dihje was more confused than ever, Spencer less so. Yet it was not in the nature of Mr. Dihje to either question the activities he was led into by Spencer or to ask for a clarification of the fruits of their efforts. Any more than it was in Spencer's nature to volunteer information. Spencer was one of those men who, when working on a crossword puzzle, wouldn't think of calling out, "Anyone know a six-letter word for wind beginning with Z?"* He considered any case he undertook to be a personal challenge, and while he relied on his assistant for help in the investigation, he rarely undertook to speculate on his conclusions before they were proved.

For his part, Mr. Dihje, curiously, had relatively little interest in a case's resolution. His enjoyment came from the process more than the result. He trusted in Spencer's ability to keep them moving on a constructive course of action, and enjoyed the ride without looking toward the future.

At Geary and Fillmore, Spencer turned right and scanned the street ahead for an address. He pulled the Legacy over to the curb and angled the car into a convenient parking space. They got out, locked the car, and walked to a doorway next to a storefront. Then they mounted the steps to the second-floor offices of the Conrad Custom Carpentry Company.

It is not necessary to follow the duo inside and witness a second improvisation. As we have seen, it was Spencer's habit to avoid identifying himself whenever possible, as in many unfamiliar situations one does not know what hidden guilt will be triggered, apropos of the crime under consideration or other-

* (Zephyr)

wise, when the word "detective" is uttered. In this case, he represented himself as a homeowner with a kitchen to be remodeled who had been recommended to the firm by Mr. Wilkesford Harrington.

Our remaining outside might, in fact, be of greater use to the investigative effort, for Spencer's sensibilities could easily be upset were he to return and find his fine automobile diminished. In fact, no sooner had he and Mr. Dihje disappeared upstairs than the street's inhabitants entered into a discussion of the value of the automobile's hubcaps.

The situation was saved by a propitious glance out the window by Mr. Dihje. He opened the window, leaned out, and gave his best imitation of Fu Manchu. The car's admirers smiled and returned to other pursuits.

In due course, Spencer thanked the administrative assistant to the proprietor of the Conrad Custom Carpentry Company, and they returned to the car and made their way home.

Probably you are wondering why this awkward stop had been inserted in the otherwise distinguished itinerary. Spencer had obtained the name of the small free-lance construction firm which the Harringtons' wedding coordinator had employed to build the platform upon which the ill-fated groom and others in the wedding party had stood. Conrad was that firm, and had provided Spencer with the names of four carpenters employed to nail the thing together. Three of them would be of no interest to you, as they were not to Spencer. The fourth was Frederick Marchand, eldest son of the department store mogul Carl, and late of the San Francisco Opera Company, backstage division. Many people, it seems, hold down two jobs these days.

Chapter 15

A Chekhovian gun in the third act.

Due to the impending climax, we will pass over dinner, which Mr. Dihje stir-fried from an odd assortment of leftover vegetables, and advance directly to the shank of the evening, when Spencer and Mr. Dihje arrive on foot at a small marble table on the sidewalk of downtown Broadway, the galleria of one Enrico. Spencer sported a beret for the occasion. Louis, wearing his habitual brown suit, sat nursing a cup of Cappuccino. At a nearby table covered with makeup and wigs, two young men were halfway through the process of turning themselves into young women. Or perhaps two young women were turning themselves into young men. Louis couldn't be sure. He tore his eyes away.

"Hi, Mr. Holmes. How's the investigation going?"

"It draws quickly to a conclusion. More and more pieces of the puzzle tumble into place. The gun, in fact, is one of the few remaining that haven't. What do you have for us?"

"This guy we're going to meet, he sold what you're looking for to a single male, about thirty-five, sparse hair, potbelly, aproximately five foot eight. About ten days ago. The contact was made through a friend. Apparently the guy was willing to shell out a wad for a first-class weapon and a scope and he put the word out on the street. My contact thought he knew the one man who could supply a gun like that, and I ran him down last night. I had to promise we wouldn't hassle him. He doesn't come out of his hole ordinarily, and he doesn't know his customer's name and hasn't seen him since."

"Very interesting. Let's go see your friend."

Louis paid his bill and the three walked down the street to a small storefront with its windows painted over in red Day-Glo paint. Silhouettes featured voluptuous females in exotic positions.

"Good evening, gentlemen, no cover, no minimum, continuous showings, our girls have no inhibitions whatsoever . . ."

"Save it." Louis stopped the man's spiel and they went inside.

The room was dark and foggy with cigarette smoke. It took some seconds for their eyes to adjust to the available light. Louis led them to a purple-upholstered booth in the back, where they slipped in. A forty-year-old woman tottering on high heels, bulging through mesh tights, and scratching underneath her naked breasts appeared at their side carrying a cork tray. Louis ordered three Singapore Slings. Spencer began to protest. Louis held up his hand.

"They don't serve Perrier water here, Mr. Holmes. And we don't want to attract undue attention."

Unaware that he ever attracted attention, Spencer deferred to the operative. They waited.

On the stage a woman was walking back and forth, seemingly unaware of either the small crowd or the music. She wore a negligee trimmed with the fur of something which would never be defended by the League for the Preservation of Rare Species. After a chorus or two of music, she opened it in the front, revealing a mismatched bra and panties. She made a few passes with the bottom of the negligee over the bald head of a man at a front table, then took it off and tossed it toward the wings, where it fell on the floor at the edge of the stage.

Spencer looked over the room. Three tables were occupied, including theirs. One man sat at the bar.

"He ain't here yet. But he'll come. I promised him two hundred bucks."

Spencer looked back at the stage.

The girl had shrugged off her bra and was kneading her breasts. Her eyes glazed over. Whatever she was thinking about, it wasn't her performance. Next she stripped off her underwear. Left with only a G-string and high-heel shoes, she went through a series of Jane Fonda exercises on the floor.

A man silently slid into the booth beside Louis. Spencer turned his attention away from the spectacle onstage. No one shook hands. Spencer opened the conversation.

"You," began Spencer with authority, "sell guns on the black market?"

The man had the face of a ferret. A thin black beard outlined his mouth. Gold chains dangled from both wrists. A purple satin shirt blended in with the upholstery. He looked around hastily, wiped his forehead with two fingers, looked back at Louis, then shifted his eyes to the drink in front of Spencer. His voice slipped out through his nostrils.

"Not me, professor. I don't sell nothin' on the black market. I teach kindergarten, you got it?"

"Yes, I think so." Spencer pulled an envelope out of his pocket. He extracted the photo of Harry Pearl he had obtained during his interview with Pearl's girlfriend.

"Is this man in your class?" He laid it faceup on the table and slid it across. The man picked it up. He took a book of matches from the ashtray and lit one, holding it next to the small photo. It burned down to his fingers. At the last minute he blew it out.

"I seen him before."

"Doing what?"

"Doing business."

"Whose?"

"I don't know you."

Spencer took a small card out of his pocket, a business card that gave his name and address. He laid it on the table and turned it over. He withdrew a thin gold Mark Cross pen from his inside breast pocket, wrote a name and a telephone number on the back, and slid it across the table in the tracks of the photograph.

"Call this number. Tell him I want your help."

When the man lifted the card to his eyes, they widened. He looked at Spencer with renewed respect. Then his eyes narrowed again.

He slipped out of the booth and went to a pay phone. Louis watched him. Spencer and Mr. Dihje watched the stage. The girl had been replaced by another girl in a leopard-skin leotard. She had wrapped herself around a pole at the edge of the stage and was performing a lascivious imitation of a fireman's descent.

The man returned. Spencer looked up.

"I trust my references are satisfactory," Spencer asked.

The man slid silently back into the booth. He appeared contrite. His manner was far more cooperative.

"This guy's a dead ringer for the one who bought the rifle. It was a bolt-action, clip-fed Mannlicher-Carcano."

"The Oswald weapon. The bastard." Spencer's normally placid face darkened in anger.

"He paid $2,000 in twenties. He wanted it unregistered, with the serial numbers filed. He had some connections and must have asked around. I heard about it from a guy I know who only handles handguns."

"Where did you get it?"

"That oughta be a trade secret."

"Professional courtesy. I'm not interested in you or the gun, just the man."

"Mail order, a place in Chicago. You can find a bunch of them in the back of *American Gunman*."

"But your name is on the gun."

"It's a phony, and a drop address. Then I file the numbers. I send a money order in a false name, in advance."

"An entrepreneur for the times, encouraging the rising tide of violence."

"I don't tell anyone what to do with their guns. We got a right to bear arms in this country."

"We have lost that right through our own irresponsibility. Besides, the redcoats aren't coming any longer."

Spencer turned his attention to the stage, and the interview came to an end. The man took an envelope from Louis and left without the usual amenities.

On the stage a third woman had taken her turn. Entirely naked but for spiked heels, she paraded back and forth while covering and uncovering her sensitive areas with a fan, which she provocatively opened and closed as she strategically turned her back. Spencer idly admired the choreographic ingenuity of the act.

As the woman left the stage to desultory applause, Spencer, Louis, and Mr. Dihje took the opportunity to quit the theatrical establishment. On the sidewalk under the neon lights of Broadway they separated, Louis to return to the office and Spencer and his partner to their home.

Just before retiring for the evening, Spencer made an entry into his computer.

"The gun was purchased by Harry Pearl, nee Harris Perlmutter, late-night manager of the Bald Eagle. . . . Tomorrow we crack the case."

Chapter 16

Revisiting the scene of several sisters.

Mr. Dihje was awakened before dawn by his alarm clock, which he had set with special care the night before. Accustomed to an irregular life since entering the employ of Spencer Holmes some five years earlier, he rose without protestation and performed his morning toilet. He descended to the kitchen, where Spencer was already energetically preparing whole wheat pancakes. Mr. Dihje recognized the signs of restlessness as indicative of a rapidly approaching apocalypse. He set the table and put out fresh orange juice. They breakfasted in silence, a sure sign that the revelation was near at hand, for it was only when Spencer was turning over possibilities in his mind that he enumerated them aloud. Once he had settled the puzzle for himself, he did not find any need to test the solution against the opinions of others. Instead, he virtually dismissed it from his mind as a fait accompli. Only action was required now, and Spencer felt a sense of satisfaction that he had ferreted out the key riddle of the case.

Just after Mr. Dihje had cleared the table and put the dishes into the dishwasher, Spencer returned with a small black bag commonly referred to in low circles as a burglar's kit. He led the way to the garage, where they stowed the bag in the trunk of the inconspicuous Volkswagen, and drove to the rear alley of the Sisters of Mercy Orphanage.

They got out of the car and stood under the window. Mr. Dihje accurately threw a small iron grappling hook onto the windowsill overhead, then pulled taut the rope attached to it. He scrambled up the side of the ancient brick building, and with one hand holding himself in place and both feet planted on the wall, he withdrew a small tool resembling a can opener from his jacket, wedged it between the frame of the double-sash window, and slipped the latch. Then he lifted the lower pane and stepped into the room. Immediately Spencer raced up the rope and followed him inside.

The detective went straight for the file cabinet that had yielded up the adoption information on Felicity Bernstein. He withdrew three files on a hunch that he could avoid a repeat of the lengthy process of examining them all: the Felicity Bernstein/Harrington file and one from either side.

The first was the adoption records of Jose Louis Alonzo.

The second file was the adoption record of Mark Shawn, the son of Sarah Bernstein.

"Twins. Fraternal twins. Just as I surmised. The key to my recognizing the face of Mark Shawn, tennis pro. I had seen him twice before. Once at the wedding, and once in the face of Felicity Bernstein."

Chapter 17

In which the detective deduces the manner of the crime, leaving only the principal loose end for a later date.

Upon returning to the mansion on Baker Street, Spencer closeted himself in his study pursuing a series of telephone calls. A meeting was arranged for an hour hence at Mr. Harrington's Belvedere estate, to include only Harrington himself, Chief Kelly, and Spencer—ably assisted by his man, of course.

Delaying only long enough to assure himself a dramatic entrance, he drove across the Golden Gate Bridge, circled Sausalito, and wheeled through the gates of the Belvedere estate ten minutes late. There he dismissed the Pinkerton guards, instructing them that the young lady under their watch was no longer in any danger, and they vacated the premises. Spencer and Dihje were escorted by the butler to the office of Wilkesford Harrington, where they were ushered into the presence of the head of homicide and the lord of the manor.

"Good morning, Wilkesford. Good morning, Chief. I hope I haven't kept you waiting."

"You have kept us in suspense, Spencer," the Chief said facetiously. She had put in several fifteen-hour days on this case to no avail, and Spencer's promise to reveal the identity of the murderer had been made with too much self-assurance for the competitive Ms. Kelly. Needless to say, the Chief, who had risen to her present position by virtue of successfully cracking a number of cases that had confounded her male counterparts, found her position frustrating. On the other hand, she admired the detective, and if he could satisfactorily explain the current conundrum she would be impressed and ultimately delighted to move on to some other inquiry. Besides, Spencer had a reputation for eschewing credit where credit was due, and it was his practice to allow the official arm of society to make the appropriate statements to the media.

"You may recall," began Spencer, "that our unfortunate young man was nailed—excuse me, shot—just behind the right ear. This led us to believe that the shot came from the general direction of the house or grounds, a conviction that was reinforced by the near impossibility of a shot being fired from either the assemblage of guests or beyond. Notice that I used the qualifier "near." According to the eyewitness account of the maid of honor, whose gaze was naturally riveted on the young couple with all the concentration of both a participant in the drama and an envious young romantic, at the precise moment of the shooting, the groom, in fact, had his head turned directly toward his future wife. He was, as we were informed, whispering some common words of endearment. This gives rise to a whole new theory, that the shot was fired neither from the house nor the grounds. We are therefore encouraged to admit the possibility of the shot originating from the Bay. In fact, that is exactly what happened."

In deference to Mr. Holmes, both Harrington and Kelly silently considered his theory. Harrington, giving him the benefit of the doubt, framed his question as favorably as he could.

"Is that possible?"

"It is. It was done through the open porthole of a yacht with a high-powered rifle, and with the use of two instruments of high-tech practicality: a rifle scope and a Steadicam."

"A what?" Kelly blurted out.

"A Steadicam. I'm sure if the overworked Chief Kelly were free to peruse magazines devoted to the craft of filmmaking, which is a regular custom of mine, it would have occurred to her as well. It is a device which allows a motion picture camera to be strapped to the body of a cameraman. It is weighted, balanced, and swiveled in a more complex variation of the gyroscope, thereby allowing the lens to maintain an exactly perpendicular attitude to the ground, and therefore the horizon. It was invented in 1974 by Garret Brown and first utilized in a feature film by the cinematographer Haskell Wexler for a most elegant shot in *Bound for Glory*. It allows, and here is the key, a hand-held camera to have the steadiness of a tripod. Hence its name. On a calm day, it can easily counter the erratic rolling movement of a ship. Then it's a simple matter of replacing the camera with the weapon. You will also recall that no one was overly startled by a gunshot. This is because of the distance it traveled and the muffling effect water has on sound."

"This is fantastic. It's pure science fiction."

"Indeed it is, Mr. Harrington. But you will agree, I think, that we certainly live in the age of science fiction. We have traveled past Orwell's 1984, are well within sight of the 2001 of Kubrick—a filmmaker who has made extensive use of the Steadicam for purposes of the macabre, I might add—and have seen the wildest imaginings of Jules Verne and H. G. Wells come to life. We can fly to the far corners of the solar system, observe the darkest recesses of the universe itself. Yes, Mr. Harrington, this assassination was a work of science fiction. Carried out with surprising ease. Man's inventions have always been greedily seized upon by evil forces as well as good ones."

Chief Kelly had kept silent until now.

"I don't want to seem curmudgeonly, Spencer, but exactly where is the evidence for this theory?"

"Unfortunately, the weapon is, I'm quite certain, at the bottom of the Bay. Whether the weapon was jettisoned immediately or, more likely, thrown overboard some distance from the scene, we have no way of knowing. But speaking of science fiction, it might be spotted with radar and brought up. Ballistics could then do its stuff. The only proof I have of the gun is an informant who identified the suspect as the purchaser of an unregistered gun which exactly fits the requirements and fires a bullet of the type found in the groom's skull. He took possession of the gun the day before the murder. On this same day, a Steadicam was rented from Cinema Rentals for the weekend."

"And it's the same man?"

"No, it's two men. Excuse me—five, to be exact."

"A conspiracy of five men? All to murder an innocent boy?"

"No, to prevent the impending marriage of your daughter, which would have caused an inheritance amounting to more than a million dollars to slip out of their hands forever."

At this point a small cacophony overcame the proceedings. Spencer, anxious to lay out his story in its entirety, continued to speak. Chief Kelly, anxious to bring the name of a suspect into the conversation, demanded the identity of the five men.

Harrington questioned the existence of an inheritance, as he was, he had assumed, the only fiscal feature of the girl's future. Realizing the ineffectiveness of simultaneous conversation, the small audience quieted. Spencer laid out the following.

"One Stephen Douglas Turner, Jr. masterminded the conspiracy. He is a competent chess player and murder-mystery buff. As he was the only one of the five who had managed to keep his substantial inheritance intact, I believe his motivation stemmed from a fantastic desire to construct and carry out the perfect crime. He enlisted the help of the others, all of whom were in various stages of financial disarray, but had acquired a taste for money as the descendants of wealthy San Franciscans. Probably they were easy to convince for that reason.

"Harry Pearl, born Harris Perlmutter, manager of a disreputable topless nightclub, was in contact with the sleazier San Francisco elements, and obtained the gun. His photo was identified last night by the black-market gunsmith who sold it to him. Robert Hansen was a small-time filmmaker who rented and then returned the Steadicam through his production company. Since saltwater has an effect on delicate equipment of this nature, we might identify the pieces under microscopic examination. Randal Fleischakel provided, and probably captained, his yacht, the *Bacchus*. I'm certain a conversation with the denizens of the Marina Green harbor will establish that it put to sea Sunday afternoon. Sundays, however, there are literally hundreds of boats in the water. All of this was meticulously arranged well in advance of the crime, after which the mastermind went away for some months, returning shortly after the wedding, in order to have a cast-iron alibi. The bride had announced her marriage for June 15. Turner knew that on June 16, a fortune would slip through his fingers. He formulated the plan as he did because, I believe, he wanted to wait to the last possible moment, in the event that it would become unnecessary. After all, more than one marriage has been canceled at the eleventh hour, and perhaps he had no real desire to murder an innocent young man."

Kelly raised her hand.

"You said there were five men. That's only four."

"It was necessary that the platform be positioned in the most advantageous way. Freddy Marchand was a stagehand and free-lance carpenter who managed to get himself work on its construction. It would have been his job to see that there were no obstructions between the platform and the Bay, and that its height permitted clear access over the seated guests."

"Which one of them pulled the trigger?"

"That, I'm afraid to say, we shall never know. Nevertheless, they are equally responsible in the eyes of the law."

"Pardon me for sounding like a defense attorney, but aren't the activities of these men pretty circumstantial?" Harrington interjected.

"I'm afraid I must agree with you. Now that the event has passed, it is almost impossible to prove culpability. That is where motivation rears its ugly head."

"The inheritance?"

"That's right. Because of the eccentric bequest of *their* fathers, each of whom believed himself to be the natural father of Miss Felicity, they would receive the substantial trust fund only if she failed to meet the terms of the will: that she be married prior to her twenty-first birthday. That was the unusual condition of an unusual will that was the result of an unusual alliance. On the other hand, if she were married in time, the money would be hers."

"And if not, the men would collect a million dollars?"

"Not exactly. We come now to the most curious aspect of the trust. It was a tontine, which stays intact until the last surviving legatee collects it. An old-fashioned, obscure codicil with the singular feature of insuring envy and greed, and perhaps even mayhem, among its recipients. Of the five men, four had to die before the fifth could collect it. Turner may have had some plans in that direction; I would not put it past him. However, it is most likely that, as the attorney, he promised the men the trust could be broken and each would collect $200,000."

"And they probably will," Kelly said, looking exceedingly glum. "You have means, motive, and opportunity. But we haven't any proof. Maybe they'll break down," she said hopefully. "We'll separate them—"

"That," Spencer interjected quietly, "has already been accomplished. Each man has passed away in his own time. His own *good* time, I think we can agree."

"What!" Harrington exclaimed. "They're all dead?"

"As doornails, to strain an old cliche."

"Wait a minute," Kelly said. "These are the same men you told me about last week?"

"The very same."

"And you believed them murdered, if I recall?"

"I do."

"All five? And just who is responsible for that?"

"For the deaths of Harry Pearl, Harold Fleischakel, Robert Hansen, and Freddy Marchand, the mastermind Stephen Douglas Turner, Jr. was responsible. He had no intention of sharing the money with his accomplices, though the money was less important than his desire to complete the perfect crime. Turner was the only one of the five who had increased rather than lost his inheritance. He knew they had squandered theirs, and preyed on their need for money. After the first two were dead, Hansen and Marchand arranged a meeting, suspecting something. When we saw Marchand at Hansen's, he told us he was just arriving. But he was probably leaving, after they had planned Turner's murder. Marchand, left to carry it out alone, did so by injecting poison in Turner's Scotch earlier in the day. Then he went on to his job at the opera, where he was killed by Turner. Later in the evening, after an interview I conducted with him, Turner drank the poisoned Scotch and died instantly. And voilà, all five are murdered by each other. Poetic justice."

Spencer's explanation was followed by a long silence. Due to the lack of living culprits, the climax was unsatisfactory to all those present. Harrington, for one, wanted a warm body on which to blame the interruption of an expensive, catered affair. Chief Kelly would be unable to make an arrest, or even close the case officially, without a suspect in handcuffs.

Finally Spencer reopened the conversation.

"Your daughter is perfectly safe now. I have thought so for several days, but did not wish to take any unnecessary risks."

"I want to thank you for your work, Mr. Holmes. A great weight has been taken off my mind." Harrington didn't appear to be the lighter for the conversation. "By the way, did you uncover Felicity's natural parents in the course of your work?"

"Felicity's natural father passed away not long after she was born. I've tracked down her mother. She has respected your rights and has never expected to see Felicity. I leave all that up to you. I might only say that she is a remarkable woman. It might be troubling to your daughter to know that her natural mother was the mistress of five men in a complex arrangement, the details and history of which will be in my confidential report. You will have to use your own judgment. And your daughter will need hers as well. The name and address will be in the report, and you and she can decide whether to pursue it or not. I will messenger it to you in the morning, along with my bill."

There were the normal amenities, and the detective stood and shook hands with Mr. Harrington. Finally he and Kelly walked down the front drive, with Mr. Dihje following at a discreet distance behind.

"Pardon me for questioning your eminence, Spencer, but are you absolutely sure of all this?"

"Quite. You'll find the will on file with the firm of Turner, Bachman and Turner. A million dollars, you'll agree, can be a powerful motivation. The yacht is at slip 17, Marina Green. Hansen Productions, now being dismantled by its secretary, has a receipt for the equipment. Conrad Custom Carpentry hired the carpenter, and has no reason to deny it. You'll have to take our word for the gun; I promised my contact anonymity. All circumstantial, as you pointed out; but irrefutable, I think. You might run down the telephone records of the five men. They professed not to know each other, but some sort of communication must have existed."

"It really doesn't matter now, does it?"

"No, it doesn't. I was just trying to give you confidence in me."

"Something you have never lacked in yourself."

On that note, they shook hands and parted. Kelly drove away in her black-and-white. Spencer walked to his own car, where Mr. Dihje waited patiently.

"Mr. Turner, weighing a great deal, is unlikely candidate for climbing around backstage opera, I think." Mr. Dihje eyed Spencer suspiciously.

"Ah yes. I thought you raised your eyebrows a tad when I came to that particular hole in my explanation. I ought to tell you now that some of my recent explanations were not altogether true. Although the men plotted and executed the death of the unfortunate young man for no other reason than to prohibit the marriage, they did not kill each other. We have another stop to make before this case is wrapped up. There is a murderer on the loose, and we are on his trail now."

Chapter 18

Finale Ultimo, or, the steaming scenario ends.

Naked and alone, Spencer Holmes sat on the middle tier of a white-tiled steam room. The steam swirled thickly around him. This is how it must have been for my grandfather on the London streets, he thought. Not being able to see beyond a foot or two. Not knowing who or what would suddenly appear out of the mist. The next figure, looming up without any warning, could be a friend or a foe. It might be a madman, or a murderer. In any event, his resourceful grandfather had been prepared, and he resolved to be the same.

He heard the glass door swing open and shut again. The slap of naked feet on wet tile echoed in the chamber, confusing the pattern of their approach. Then, suddenly, a tall, muscular figure passed in front of him.

"Mark Shawn, isn't it?"

The young man turned and peered back at Spencer. He put on his club-pro personality.

"Yes, hello." He extended his hand and they shook.

"Spencer Holmes. I was here last weekend. I played Sarah Bernstein. We met briefly in the shop."

"I remember. How did you do?"

"I lost, I'm afraid. A bit humiliating."

"Oh, I wouldn't be embarrassed, if I were you. Sarah is an outstanding player. Always does well in club tournaments."

"You've been teaching her?"

"Coaching her. She learned the game some time ago, before I was born."

"Yes, exactly. Before you were born."

Only the hiss of the steam sounded in the room.

"You've become a member, then," Shawn said. "I'm sure you will enjoy it. The tennis is on a very high level, and the facilities are excellent."

"Actually, I'm just a guest of Wilkesford Harrington. Perhaps you know him?"

"Yes, I think so."

Shawn stood erect, with his feet apart, naked, his hands gripping a rolled towel around his neck. Wary of each other, their eyes locked. When you want to know what a man does, Spencer thought, look at his hands. When you want to know who a man is, look at his face. But when you want to know what a man will do, look in his eyes.

Shawn climbed to the top tier and sat behind Spencer's left shoulder.

"How was your game today?" Spencer inquired.

"Fine. And yours?"

"Afoot."

"I don't think I understand."

"I'm sorry, it is a colloquial expression. Before your time, I think."

"Ah."

More silence. Drops of water fell from the ceiling and splashed on the tile floor. They echoed in the steam room. A faint smell of eucalyptus drifted through the steamy air.

"It's late," Shawn said. "And I didn't see you playing this afternoon."

"No. I just arrived. Came for the steam. Wonderfully invigorating. Well, the fact is, it was I who sent you the note, asking to meet you here."

"You'd like to arrange some coaching? I don't have my book with me, but I'm sure we can fit you in."

"Not exactly. Not that my game couldn't use help. But just now I wanted to speak to you about a few things. I think," Spencer ventured, "that you are somewhat more than you appear to be."

Mark Shawn waited, then quietly spoke.

"I am a tennis player, and a student at Berkeley."

"And the son of Professor William Shawn?"

"Of course."

"I think not. You are the adopted son of the good professor and his wife, but the natural son of Sarah Bernstein, and the twin brother of Felicity Harrington. And what's more, I think you know it."

Spencer sensed a tension at his side rippling through the young man's powerful calf.

"Yes. That's true. But I think of William and Marguerite Shawn as my parents. They raised me from birth."

"Yet I believe you feel a certain loyalty to your blood relatives."

"I don't know what you mean."

"Your sister, for example. You have known of her existence for how long?"

"About three years. Look, I may as well tell you right out: I attended her wedding."

"Yes. I saw you there, after the unfortunate interruption. You were invited?"

"Not exactly. A friend of mine knows Felicity and received an invitation. I was her guest."

"How convenient for you."

"I admit I manipulated the situation. I wanted to see her get married. It's not a crime."

"A crime is precisely what took the place of the wedding."

"I didn't kill him. That's ridiculous. You can ask my date."

"I don't have to. I know you didn't. But you must admit your actions are eccentric."

"All right, I'll tell you the story. A little over three years ago, when I turned eighteen, I went to court and petitioned for the right to know my real parents. It was a natural curiosity, which many adopted children have. The court granted me the name of my mother from the adoption agency."

"And you found Sarah Bernstein and introduced yourself?"

"Yes. That's all."

"Oh no it isn't, I don't believe."

"Sarah and I liked each other right away. We were tentative at first, but we get along very well. She eventually told me about Felicity, and we agreed for the time being not to say anything. If Felicity wanted to, she could do what I had done."

"And she told you about your father."

"My fathers. I know all about that. It was all before I was born. Sarah explained it to me. But she needn't defend herself, not to me, and not to you, either. I'm not such a prude as to make a big deal of it."

Spencer reflected on the sensibilities of the young. Then he came to his ace card.

"No, your father. Singular. Not one of the five men, but Matthew Adler, this club's builder and Sarah Bernstein's tennis coach, and weekend lover. And one true love."

The young man didn't speak at once. When he did it was cautiously.

"You don't know that. No one does."

"You do. And I think Sarah does as well. She would certainly have seen the resemblance by the time you were eighteen. I've seen your father's picture at the clubhouse. What I don't know is how you established it. Did she tell you?"

There was another long pause, and when the boy spoke this time he seemed almost relieved. A door to his heart had been opened. The words tumbled out faster now.

"Both. She pointed out the resemblance and I took the necessary steps to establish it for certain. It was luck really, but it's irrefutable. Blood type."

"Of course. Ingenious of you."

"I had a serious injury in my freshman year, and discovered that I had a rare blood type, AB-positive. Out of curiosity, I checked my real mother's and researched the others'. She was A."

"The second most common."

"Yes. But by coincidence, the men were all O or A. None of the A's were RH-positive. You see?"

"I do. What about Adler?"

"B-positive."

"Your biology teacher must have been quite proud. What did you do with all this information?"

"Nothing. I was interested, and now I know."

"But surely the five men provided fertile ground for your investigations?"

"Once I found out that none of them were my real father, I had no interest. They were nothing to me."

"On the contrary, you harbor an intense grudge. Shall I tell you what they did to your father?"

Mark Shawn hesitated, sighed, and finally spoke.

"No. All right. I know about that. But Sarah doesn't. I came across their names in my father's papers and a diary, which

Sarah had put away in a safe-deposit box, but never looked at. I discovered they were his investors. They must have found out about my father and Sarah. They were probably terribly jealous, as he was unmarried and much closer to her age. But he was an outsider. They found out about him and maneuvered him into developing these facilities, promising to provide all the necessary financing. He put up all he had, and they backed out. They ruined him financially and he never recovered. Obviously he never told Sarah that his financial problems were linked to them. Sarah loved him, but she was young and felt a lot of loyalty to the older men. She never had a father of her own, you know."

"Now about the will."

"What will?"

"Oh, we've come this far, young man, don't hold back on me now."

"I know about it. I studied the five men pretty thoroughly. And when Sarah told me I was a twin, I looked up the legal documents."

"I am surprised you were not mentioned in it."

"Something Sarah told me explained that. The fact is, the five men never suspected twins, and Sarah never told them. The adoptions were carried out through the orphanage, and, perhaps for reasons having something to do with her memory of my real father, she told them about the girl, but not her son."

Finally Spencer pointed to the fulcrum of his entire theory.

"And at the wedding, when you saw the boy shot, because of the will you knew instantly who had killed him."

It was a long time before Mark Shawn answered. Spencer waited. The room was hot and close. Sweat poured now from their bodies, which glistened in the dimly lit room. Finally Shawn spoke in a low voice.

"I did."

"And you plotted your own revenge."

Spencer felt the boy's powerful body shift slightly.

"They had to have killed him. I didn't know how, but it had to be them. They were guilty and would get away with it just the way their fathers got away with their plot to ruin my father. I couldn't let that happen. I didn't know which one did it; I thought maybe it was more than one. It didn't matter. But

Sarah had nothing to do with what I did. I wanted to kill them all, and I did. They deserved to die."

Spencer might have agreed with this, but had no opportunity to say so. Shawn did not give it to him. He had gripped his rolled towel in both hands, slipped it off his shoulders, and in an instant snaked it around Spencer's neck, pulling it tight. Just in time, Spencer slipped three fingers between the tightening noose and his neck, and simultaneously rolled forward. Together the two men slid off the platform and rolled onto the floor. The younger man maintained his grip, squeezing the ropelike towel. Spencer's breathing became more difficult and he began to lose consciousness.

At that moment, the rope eased and dropped away to the floor. Shawn fell away, unconscious. Appearing from the far corner of the steam room, dripping with sweat, was the resourceful Mr. Dihje, who had merely applied a firm finger to the appropriate spot on the tennis teacher's neck. Shawn had slipped into a deep and relaxing slumber. Side by side, Spencer and Mr. Dihje sat on the lowest platform, while Mark Shawn slept like a baby at their feet.

"There is no man I would rather have by my side in time of danger. You have saved my life. Again," Spencer said quietly. "Thank you."

But Mr. Dihje, whose concept of friendship was based on another culture in which it was a deeper and more complex relationship than in the traditional American buddy system, considered it simply his duty, and was already ruminating on another subject.

"I lose plenty weight here, I bet." Mr. Dihje smiled happily.

"Yes, Mr. Dihje. It has been invigorating for all of us, I think."

Chapter 19

In which Spencer Holmes exhibits a good deal less misogyny than his famous forebear had.

"And you didn't turn him in?" the soprano asked Spencer, her bright blue eyes widening with alarm, as they sat in the opera cafe at eleven o'clock that night. Spencer had appeared to her out of the fog as she stepped out of the stage door following her evening performance. As she had never received the attentions of a stage-door Johnny, certainly not one wearing white tie and tails and brandishing a matching cane, she was enormously pleased to see him, even though he was a week late.

"No. I felt he had acted in a good cause, however impetuous he may have been. He had tumbled to the men, knew that one or more of them had murdered the boy. He knew, too, that they would never be caught, certainly never convicted. So he took the law into his own hands. I cannot condone that, of course, although I myself have been known to do the same, when absolutely neccessary. I simply chose not to judge him too harshly. In any case, it would have been difficult to establish the guilt of all five men beyond a reasonable doubt. The plan had been too well conceived, and well executed. And probably it was too fantastic for the pedantic minds of the district attorney's office, let alone twelve good men and true. There is far too much room for reasonable doubt."

"So you let him go?"

"He has his own conscience to answer to, not mine. The case, as far as I am concerned, is concluded. In the end, the five men paid the proper price for their cold-blooded murder. They forfeited their own lives."

"It seems fantastic," she breathed.

"Nevertheless, I assure you that every word of the case is

absolute fact, on my honor as a gentleman." Spencer suddenly regretted his last remark, in the event that, later, his honor as a gentleman might be tested by this bewitching and musical creature and found wanting. "Except the names, of course. They have been changed to protect your innocence."

She blushed.

"Right now, may I suggest we repair to the Sheraton on Post Street. There is a cozy bar at the top in which we might partake of a nightcap. It has a room I'd like you to see. A quaint facsimile of quarters I myself have some small connection with, from another place, and an extraordinary time, long, long ago."

Five minutes later, a beautiful dark-haired woman could be seen tightly holding the elbow of her escort as the two of them strolled the mean streets of present-day San Francisco.

If you enjoyed Spencer Holmes and Sowhat Dihje in SAN FRANCISCO KILLS, *you will enjoy their second outing in which they track down a very wily murderer.*

The following is a sample of KILLER FIN-ISH, *Bantam's second novel by Denny Martin Flinn, due out in August, 1991.*

Chapter 1:   Prestidigitation and Mayhem

The audience did not appreciate the magician. You could feel it in the very air. His opening levitation—the girl floating over his head and spinning on her trim axis—failed to elicit awe. *The greatest opening since Blackstone. What do you people want?*

A flock of doves launched from his pearl-handled cane fell on deaf ears as well. He pulled himself up straight, felt a tug in his crotch from aging tails custom-fitted to a younger version of his physique, and headed into his grabber.

This had to do it. He flashed his teeth, snapped his two-inch boot heels together, swept his arm up, turned to the wings. His assistant lunged out of the shadows pushing the long box. She parked it in front of him.

They raised their linked hands cheerily toward the audience. She posed on one mesh-hosed leg, tottered on the stiletto heel. He opened the top. He reached down and slipped his hand under her ass to help her in. *Nice.* She climbed gracefully into the box, simultaneously slapping his hand off her bottom. She slipped her feet through the holes at one end and her head through a hole at the other. She lay on her back before him.

His eyes glided admiringly over her prone anatomy. Her chest strained against the sequined bodice. A drop of perspiration rolled off the top of her breast and headed down toward her neck. A patch of skin showed between the gilded Merry Widow bodice and her tight shorts, exposing her belly button and a soft, peach-fuzzed abdomen that pushed against the top of her tights. Black mesh hose threaded her trim legs.

For a moment the magician was reminded of his triumphant South American tour, when he'd had several assistants, each one lovely and ripe. He had visited as many of their rooms every night as he had time and strength to do. His glory days.

He closed the box. She smiled and wiggled her feet at the audience. *This should get them.* He stepped back to his black and brass wardrobe trunk and pulled out a menacing chrome chain saw. He waved it overhead. He dropped it down to waist level and yanked the chain.

The motor didn't catch. For a moment he was flustered. He yanked it again. A dying sputter. He muttered under his breath. He smiled at the audience. He gave it a hard tug and it roared to life. *Thank Christ. I wouldn't have had the strength to pull it again.*

He stepped up behind the box and waved the thundering chain saw over her body. He lined up the murderously revolving blade and lowered it slowly. He strained to hear the traditional collective intake of breath from the audience.

Silence.

Where did this crowd come from Hayward?

He held the motor at maximum rpm's with his trigger finger. The saw floated gracefully through the box and dropped out the bottom. He shut it down, put it back in the prop box.

He separated the two halves, stepped between the girl's upper and lower torso. He turned them lengthwise and faced her head and her feet toward the audience. The head smiled, and the feet wiggled.

That would show them! I wowed them with that in New York City, killed them in London, startled them in Madrid!

Nothing.

It was going to be a long night.

From then on it was all downhill. He lost his rhythm. His arthritic hands lacked their renowned dexterity. His timing stumbled, causing infinitesimal but inexcusable flaws. He had performed this same routine for twenty years on seven continents. And now it wasn't going well. It wasn't going well at all.

He worried that he should not have accepted the engagement. Perhaps to think that, nearly six years after his last farewell appearance, he would be able to glide through the series of large illusions without mishap, had been a folly. Now the lights he had so enjoyed bathing in for two decades seemed harsh and unyielding. Flop sweat broke out on his brow. He blinked salty drops off his eyelashes.

The Great Gandolfo was angry. He had accepted this special one-night-only, out-of-retirement engagement because he was assured by the promoter that the house would be packed. It wasn't. He had been promised an audience of aficionados. They weren't. The promoter said the man who had arranged the performance was a longtime fan of Gandolfo who insisted on putting him back on the stage. Whoever that person was, he hadn't even sent a good luck telegram to Gandolfo's dressing room before the show. The dressing room was another sore point. No champagne. No flowers. A cold slab floor, peeling pipes overhead, the whole tiny room grimy and painted black.

He had dusted off his ancient props, oiled and polished them. He had rehearsed for a month. He had found a new assistant, taught her everything, and bought her a costume, picking it out himself from the theatrical house on Mason. He had lain awake nights negotiating, with himself to be sure, for an extension of his agreement. *One night, hell. When the public gets the story that the Great Gandolfo is back, when they see that the act is as breathtaking as ever, why, I'll run months at the club. Follow that with a tour on the West Coast. Work my way east via the Palmer House in Chicago, end up in New York City. Was the Hippodrome still there? The latest thing in Broadway. A one-man show.*

The silence that followed his Floating Ball brought him back to earth. The lack of audience response was depressing. And so was this special engagement into which he had allowed himself to be booked. For a meager sum, a fraction of his original fee. *Damn it, don't they know who the Great Gandolfo is?*

Apparently not. With the exception of one polite table in the rear, the audience sat on their hands. They fidgeted. They were bored. He could almost feel outright animosity.

He ignored them through the rest of the routine. He concentrated on his assistant. *Maybe she'll go out with me after the show. We could stop for espressos and those little Italian pastries somewhere up on Columbus. I'll tell her how well she did tonight. Promise more engagements. A cruise, maybe. They still wanted magic acts on the big ships. Women found those little cabins romantic. What the hell was her name, anyway. Crissy something. Wong. No, Kwong. That's it, Crissy Kwong. She was Chinese or Korean. Maybe Asian. They were all over the goddamn city now.*

The girl handed him the loaded top hat, and jogged him out of his reverie.

The escape went okay. He was out of the straightjacket and behind the stage before the box caught fire. And he ran through the little riffs smoothly: the linking rings, the silk dyeing, the flowers from the frying pan, the goldfish-into-Siamese cat. He skipped the mentalist routine. *I don't dare drag one of these stiffs onto the stage. Cut to the Metamorphosis.*

She brought out the stool. He stood on it, trying to resurrect some of the old bravado, flashing his cape in the air. Turned his back to the audience, extended his arms behind him, wrists together. She put the handcuffs on him. *Not so fucking tight.* He faced the audience. She blindfolded him, climbed down and fastened on the anklecuffs, chained them to the chair leg. He could feel her demonstrate the job by tugging on the chains.

She slipped his cape off his shoulders. Flared it out until it was almost double the expected length. Draped in over his head until he was entirely hidden underneath, a ghostly, headless phantom rising from the center of the stage.

"One!" the magician called out. The audience didn't seem to care.

"Two!" he called. *I know you're out there, you bastards. They didn't set up all those little red-checked tablecloths with those fucking little candles for nothing.*

"Three!" the assistant shouted in her light voice, and dropped the cape, revealing herself standing on the stool, her ankles and wrists cuffed.

The magician walked out from the wings on the far side of the stage, expecting acknowledgment. It was quieter than ever. Enthusiastic applause reverberated from one table at the rear only. *Well, at least somebody out there is a connoisseur. Someone is aware that the legendary Gandolfo Meta-*

morphosis had just been successfully executed, with split-second timing, for the first time in half a decade. Either no one else in the room knew the illusion's reputation—the first midair substitution in magic history, invented nearly forty years ago, drawing admiration from the elite circle of brother magicians—or no one cared. Odd.

Mincing steps carried him to center stage, where the girl waited on the stool. He reached into his pocket for the key. He unlocked her cuffs, helped her off the stool, and presented her to the audience unbound. She whisked her blindfold off.

They bowed.

No response. *What the hell do you want? That was my most famous trick. Don't you know I just did a Metamorphosis without covering the legs of the chair. Right there in midair, for Christ sakes. Philistines.*

The assistant skipped off into the wings.

Oh, what's the use? I'll sell all this junk and give up the act for good. There must be a lot of young magicians hungry for first-rate equipment. You couldn't find stuff this good anymore. Handmade out of the best ivory and the finest woods, inlaid with colorful crystals, solid brass fasteners. I ought to get a pretty penny.

He slipped off his tailcoat and draped it over the prop box. *Only one more trick. Thank God. The big finish.* He unbuttoned his vest and took it off. *Should I strip right down to my bare chest? That had once drawn some eager looks from the ladies, I had the body of an Adonis then. Built myself up with weights. Oiled my chest before each performance. Women had waited outside the stage door in those days.*

Not tonight. He knew his gray hairs curled limply on his fleshy breasts now. He'd leave his shirt on. He sighed. It would all be over soon.

His assistant reappeared from the wings, clicking her heels on the hard floor as she wheeled the famous Cabinet of Swords to the center of the stage.

He took hold of it and whirled it around. He opened all four sides and the top, previewing the space inside. He climbed in.

The girl closed the sides of the cabinet around him, locking them with padlocks at the edges. She lowered the top, fitting his head through a hole in the panel. When the cabinet was closed, only his head stuck out, like an old-fashioned one-man sauna. She locked the top panel to the front panel. She paraded around the stage, circling him. *Let's get this over with.* She drew the rack of swords down center. She pulled one off the rack. Light bounced off the shaft, burst, and sparkled over the audience. She waved it in the air.

She walked over to the prop table, took up a cantaloupe, placed in on the cabinet top next to his head. She swung the sword heavily. The cantaloupe split, the two halves thudded to the stage floor. She stood directly behind the magician holding the sword straight up overhead, poised like a character in a dungeons and dragons film.

Is it my imagination, or did the audience just wake up. There was a rustling in the seats, though whether they had finally been intrigued by the act, or were looking for their coats in preparation for a quick exit, he couldn't know.

Nor would he ever know. A moment later he felt a sharp sensation in the back of his neck. His body went numb. His head, neck, and vocal cords were pinioned in place. His eyes opened wide. He cast his eyes down, and just saw the tip of the sword come out of the front of the box. He saw a dark red gooey substance roll down the bright steel. It looked suspiciously like blood. He could see it drip onto the green satin shoes of his assistant. He saw her muscled legs, but couldn't turn his head to see what she was doing. All this happened in a moment. His last thought was, *I'm too old for this shit.*

His eyes rolled back in their sockets, and the Great Gandolfo ended his career as only a few fortunate others have throughout theatrical history. He died on stage. Literally.

Chapter 2:   His Last Bow

The Cabinet of Swords, the ancient illusion known as the Temple of Benares, ordinarily allowed the performer to sit inside unharmed, providing, of course, that he was initiated into its mysteries. The swords were obviously not supposed to encounter, and certainly not pass through, the magician's bulk, no matter how large. We can infer this, even without being privy to its secret ourselves, from the number of magicians who continue to perform this legendary and effective illusion. This, as far as we know, is the first time in magic history it had not been performed successfully.

Gandolfo's assistant went on with the act. She selected half a dozen more swords from their display case, and accurately slid them through the predrilled holes in the cabinet, pushing hard as they encountered the resistance of his overweight frame, until they came out the other end.

When she had completely skewered the magician, the assistant stood back and posed. She was rewarded with thunderous applause and loud bravos. On that wave of energy she waved, took several steps backward, and bowed again. She turned on her heels in a rosy glow of accomplishment and headed offstage, stapping the stage manager on her way past. He came awake with a start and drew the curtain.

Downstage, Gandolfo still sat in his cabinet, his wide grin frozen on his face, immobilized by the shafts that pierced his torso in several directions. The curtain closed behind him, the colorful cabinet illuminated by footlights. He stared, sightless, straight out at the audience, the pink hue of the warming lights giving false color to what was in fact a white and bloodless head that perched atop the polished, glittering, legendary Temple of Benares.

Although the audience had been lifeless and unresponsive for the whole of the entertainment, something about this last trick had certainly caught their fancy. Now they clapped. They whistled. They shouted their appreciation. They stood up. If only the Great Gandolfo could have been seen this display of enthusiasm, his original frustration would have been much tempered, his vanity flattered, his anger mollified. But as with the artist whose paintings only rise in value on his demise, satisfaction was not to be his.

The audience continued their hue and cry until the vigor of their appreciation was depleted. Then they dressed in their coats, congratulated each other on having chosen such an outstanding example of the performance arts, exited the nightclub—many of them passing right under the moribund nose of the Great Gandolfo—and ambled out into the chilly San Francisco night.

Chapter 3: Wherein the Ordinary Celebration Customarily Following Opening Night Does Not Take Place.

The audience, clearly, was quite pleased. Any performer would leave the theatre basking in triumph.

Gandolfo, as we know, did not. He didn't leave the stage at all. He didn't even leave his awkward seat inside his famous prop. He simply sat there, encased in the polished wood frame painted a high gloss, Chinese red, and stared out of startled eyes at the empty theatre—deceased.

More than one performer, after removing their makeup and changing out of their costume, likes, on their way out of a theatre, to wander across the empty stage and stare out at the empty seats, reliving, in the calm aftermath, their glory. A small vanity, perhaps, but a traditional one. Gandolfo was not there, as we well know by now, for any such thing. He was dead, and thus far no one had had the opportunity to address the question of his removal.

The stage manager could not see anything below the main curtain after he had closed it. Why he had closed it is only slightly more complicated. Audience response to the act (which did not in any appreciable way differ from his own when he had caught it for the first time at the dress rehearsal that afternoon) had been so quiet he had fallen asleep on his stool. An hour later, awakened by the assistant's nudge, he had assumed that the act had come to a close. He jumped off his stool, grabbed the rope, and closed the curtain. He might be forgiven this cueing error, since from the awkward backstage angle from which he viewed the proceedings, it is unlikely he would have noticed anything amiss in any case.

The electrician at the back of the house took his cue from the curtain. He shut down the spotlight, brought up the permanent warming lights and the house lights, and, never one to wait on the predilections of performers to milk their bows, climbed down his ladder and left through the front door before even the audience had collected their belongings.

So by the time the audience had exited, there was no one

left to notice the small trickle of blood that dripped out of the corner of the once Great Gandolfo's mouth, still frozen in its timeless grin as he sat in front of the empty nightclub.

With two exceptions.

You'll remember there had been enthusiastic applause from one table at the rear of the club. One party had not succumbed to the majority opinion, and had politely applauded the prestidigitator's efforts. Gandolfo himself had noticed.

Two members of the congregation had enjoyed the performance immensely and, though aware that the Great Gandolfo was not quite as young and nimble as he had once been, had clapped their appreciation at the appropriate climax of each illusion nevertheless. They were not only avid followers of that ancient, mystical art of magic, they were aware of Gandolfo's formidable, if historical, reputation, and had come to the theatre specifically to see him.

Now they studied him. Somewhat confused by the final trick and Gandolfo's failure to emerge from the cabinet unscathed, they were doubly confused when the audience, who until now had reacted with little if any emotion, chose just that feat to reward him with their most enthusiastic applause. When that audience had quit the scene, these two had lingered. They picked their way cautiously between the empty tables and chairs until they stood at the very front of the house, just below the edge of the stage, not three feet from the fatal prop, and looked up at the magician's head.

They presented a striking silhouette. One, over six feet tall —a blue blood, judging from his vaguely hawklike features —wore a classic tuxedo, including white tie and tails in a custom-fit that outlined his slim figure, and polished black patent leather loafers. He had a black cape over his arm and a silk top hat in his hand. His shock of thick, unruly gray hair was almost electric. His penetrating gray eyes surveyed the magician curiously. The other, barely over five feet tall, an East Indian with slick black hair and even white teeth set off by an olive complexion, wore sandals, baggy black broadcloth slacks, a black tuxedo shirt open at the collar and not tucked in, and a rich brocade jacket inlaid with subtle jewels. His narrow eyes revealed blue pupils, rare for an East Indian, that scrutinized the box closely. Together they were altogether an eye-catching pair, even for that eccentric city's nightlife.

"Maestro?" the taller one of them ventured in a whisper.

Naturally, the magician gazed out over their heads without acknowledging their presence. The taller one raised his voice slightly.

"Mr. Gandolfo?"

Still, of course, no response.

Now the shorter one made his attempt. He reached up and rapped his fist several times, politely but firmly, on the front of the cabinet.

There was no answer.

"Something," the taller one ventured, "has gone terribly wrong. Without, I hope, seeming to appear critical of the performance, for I enjoyed it immensely, I might conjecture that the Great Gandolfo's final illusion was not accomplished with anything like his usual aplomb. Why don't you jump up there and make a quick examination?"

This the shorter man did with an agility that belied his round figure. He climbed onto the stage, stood next to Gandolfo, and placed his middle finger against the man's carotid artery, posing in silence for a moment. He gently lifted one eyelid and peered into the whites of the man's eye in search of a pupil. He reached into the folds of his garment and extracted a short stiletto. He polished the flat side of the dagger on his sleeve until it gleamed, and held it gently under Gandolfo's nose, looking, presumably, for some evidence of breath. The knife failed to fog. Finally, he looked down at his companion and slowly, a bit sadly even, shook his head. There followed a moment of silence on both their parts.

"I see," the taller man said quietly. "It does appear then that Mr. Gandolfo has suffered an irreversible mistake in the last stages of an otherwise well-conducted act. Furthermore," he went on as he glanced around, "we may be the only ones who noticed this. The remainder of the audience seems to have appreciated the finale, and gone on their way, without ever noticing this small, if fatal, alteration in the choreography."

For the next few minutes the two men stood silently in the empty room, glancing around now and then, as if some new event might shed light on their obligation, if any. None did. The room remained ghostly, the smell of cigarette smoke and liquor—that universal olfactory evidence of a cabaret—hanging in the air. A small breeze from an open door or window drifted around the room and gently pushed at the heavy main curtain. Programs littered the floor.

They stood next to the extinct entertainer. There wasn't a sound, and there wasn't the slightest evidence that anyone else was left in the building. The two men loitered about uncertainly, as how many of us would know precisely what to do when left alone with a dead body?

In point of fact, death was not unknown to these two. It was often directly connected to their vocation. But as they had come to the theatre this night in pursuit of entertainment, and never expected to be confronted with a corpse, even they might naturally be excused from leaping into purposeful activity at once.

Eventually, however, that is exactly what they would do. And thus did Mr. Spencer Holmes and Mr. Sowhat Dihje undertake, however reluctantly, an investigation of the unfortunate accident that ended prematurely the career of the magician known as the Great Gandolfo.

BANTAM MYSTERY COLLECTION

Kinsey Millhone is...

"The best new private eye." —*The Detroit News*

"A tough-cookie with a soft center." —*Newsweek*

"A stand-out specimen of the new female operatives."
—*Philadelphia Inquirer*

Sue Grafton is...

The Shamus and Anthony Award winning creator of Kinsey Millhone and quite simply one of the hottest new mystery writers around.